HER
LONE COWBOY

HER
LONE COWBOY

BY

DONNA ALWARD

 MILLS & BOON®

First published in Great Britain 2010
Large Print edition 2010
Harlequin Mills & Boon Limited,
Eton House, 18-24 Paradise Road,
Richmond, Surrey TW9 1SR

© Donna Alward 2010

ISBN: 978 0 263 21235 8

Harlequin Mills & Boon policy is to use papers that are natural, renewable and recyclable products and made from wood grown in sustainable forests. The logging and manufacturing process conform to the legal environmental regulations of the country of origin.

Printed and bound in Great Britain
by CPI Antony Rowe, Chippenham, Wiltshire

In memory of Justice and Juliana. Always loved.

Many, many thanks to Dr. Steven MacLean for lending me his expertise on medicine and the Canadian Forces, and to the ever enthusiastic, unstoppable force that is Captain Wayne Johnston of the Wounded Warriors organization.

CHAPTER ONE

THE BLADE NICKED THE SKIN, turning the shaving cream around it pink. Noah swore, rinsed the razor in the sink of hot water, angled his head and tried again.

He felt like a baby, learning everything again for the first time. Letting out a breath, he jutted his chin and swiped the blade over his jaw once more, this time the path even and smooth. It was a good thing. He had three other nicks to attest to the poor job he was doing.

He made faces, attempting to make the skin taut where he needed it to be. In the hospital, a pretty young nurse had always come around to shave him. She'd even cut his hair when he'd asked. All he'd had to do was hold the mirror. At the time he'd enjoyed the attention. But it had worn thin. He was a man used to doing things himself. The fact that a simple morning shave caused him to break out in a sweat made him angry. At himself. At the world in general.

He held the razor in midair as there was a knock on the door.

It had to be Andrew, he reasoned. No one else really knew he was back, and that was just the way he wanted it. He scraped more cream off his face, cleaning the blade in the water. Andrew, with the familiarity of being a younger brother, would let himself in. And Andrew wouldn't care about the mess around the place.

But then the knock came again and his stomach did a slow twist. What if it wasn't Andrew? He wrinkled his brow. It could be Andrew's fiancée, Jen. Jen had been with Andrew the day they'd picked him up at the airport. Noah was only *slightly* self-conscious around Jen.

A third time it sounded, and with a growl he put down the razor and grabbed a hand towel, stomping out of the bathroom. If people with two good arms couldn't open a door…or take a hint for that matter…

Holding the towel in his fingers, he reached out and turned the knob. "Keep your pants on," he commanded, and then froze.

Not Andrew. Not even Jen. Instead, the most

beautiful woman he'd seen in forever stood on his doorstep. For a moment his gaze caught on her long, dark hair, clear skin, and finally a pair of brilliant blue eyes. Her eyebrows raised, making him feel like a child caught in a tantrum. And with a huffy sound, she brushed by him carrying a cardboard box.

Noah stared at the figure which was now heading toward his very small kitchen. What the hell? Wordlessly she put the box down and started unpacking it. In his kitchen. On his countertop.

He went to slam the door and realized he would have to forgo the satisfaction. At least he'd remembered to pin up his shirtsleeve this morning. He looked back at the kitchen. The woman had stopped her unpacking and was watching him now with undisguised interest. He felt color and heat infuse his cheeks. The last thing he wanted was morbid curiosity about his condition, or worse…pity.

He affected his best scowl. "Did you come to get a good look at the cripple?"

Lily saw Noah Laramie blush, saw him struggle and then heard the harsh words. Noah was a bad-tempered bear with a chip on his shoulder the size of a brick. So far he'd yelled at her at the door and then accused her of coming here to gawk. It was just too bad for him she was used to dealing with teenagers all day, and the way Noah was looking at her right now said *belligerence covering insecurity*. Not that she could blame him. She was a complete stranger. A smile quivered at the corner of her lips. "Are you trying to scare me away?"

His mouth dropped open for the smallest second, then he put his guard back up again and scowled. "Is it working?"

"No. You need to work on your big bad wolf impression."

"Where I come from people wait to be invited in."

Lily fired straight back, "Where I come from, people don't get yelled at, at the door."

She left the supplies on the counter and went out into the living room. She gave the pinned-up sleeve where his arm used to be no more than a glance, determined not to stare. Curiosity about how it had happened burned within her, but it would be the height of impoliteness to ask. Neither Jen nor Andrew had mentioned anything about it beyond that it had happened.

She caught her breath as they seemed to square off. His build was imposing despite the obvious. Taller than his brother, Andrew, she guessed him to be at least six-two, and even though there had to have been a distinct lack of physical activity since his injury, he was still lean and muscled. His short, dark hair was a rumpled mess, and his chin was still covered in shaving cream.

Her smile blossomed completely at the sight. "It's hard to be afraid of a man whose face resembles Santa Claus."

"Dammit," he mumbled, taking the towel and hastily wiping off the remnants of white foam. "Who *are* you?"

"I'm Lily Germaine." Without thinking, she held out her hand. Only to realize that Noah did not have a right hand to shake hers with. This time it was her cheeks that flushed and she dropped the hand back to her side.

"It's all right. I forget sometimes, too."

The quietly spoken response did more to elicit her sympathy than the sight of him had.

"I'm a friend of Jen and Andrew's. They asked me to stop by."

"Why?"

She took another step forward and looked up into his face. There were patches where he'd missed with the razor, the dark stubble shadowing a strong jaw. "Jen wanted me to deliver some groceries." She hesitated for a second. "She said you found shopping difficult and could use…"

Again she faltered. Ordinary sayings now suddenly took on new meaning. The last thing she wanted to do was insult him.

"Use a hand?"

His lips were a hard line, and the dark look in his eyes nearly sent her scuttling back to her car. But he couldn't ignore the obvious. He couldn't drive himself to the grocery store, and carting bags inside would be a definite chore. She lifted her chin. "In a manner of speaking."

He dropped the towel on the top of an armchair, putting his left hand in his jeans pocket. "Let's just get it out of the way. I'm Noah Laramie, and I've lost an arm. It is what it is. No need to dance around it. Or worry about what's going to come out of your mouth."

"It's not the appendage coming *out* of my mouth that's the problem at the moment. It's the one I keep putting *in* it." She tried a hopeful smile, relieved when the hard lines of his face relaxed. Goodness, he *was* handsome when he wasn't being so sharp and abrasive.

"Jen's a mother hen," he stated. "I'm fine. So no need to bring in whatever it is you've brought in."

Lily's smile faded. Jen hadn't said anything about the resistance Lily was suddenly facing. Oh, no. Jen had said what a teasing, easygoing guy Noah had been when they had all been growing up together—a time well before Lily had come to Larch Valley. Despite his earlier frankness in speaking, she got the feeling that trying to convince him of anything was about as effective as talking to a turnip and expecting a response. Once Noah Laramie made up his mind, she doubted anyone could budge it.

"I'm also supposed to give you a ride to Lazy L today."

"Andrew will come and get me."

"Andrew had to go to Pincher Creek."

"Then Jen."

"Jen has a bakery to open, and she asked if I'd drop these things over and give you a lift. You might as well get used to it, Laramie. I'm your chauffeur, like it or not."

After one hard, brittle glare, he stalked back

down the hall toward the bathroom. "Fine. For *today*."

She heard him shutting doors—loudly—while she put away the groceries Jen had asked her to deliver. Oh, he was a tough one. She shook her head as she opened the fridge. Inside was half a brick of cheese, a bottle of ketchup, a jar of mustard and perhaps three tablespoons of milk left in a plastic jug. She sighed, then stocked the shelves with milk, fruit, fresh vegetables and several small packages of meat. What on earth was the man eating? Clearly he'd managed, because the sink was full of dirty dishes. The furniture needed a dusting, and she wondered if he'd managed to do any laundry.

There'd been no thought of turning down Jen's request, though. Jen was her best friend and she'd do anything for her.

Even if this was the first real day of summer vacation. She could have been sleeping in, drinking coffee on her patio, sunbathing in her backyard.

She sighed. It all seemed frivolous beside Noah's problems. Losing an arm in combat and then coming home after so many years away… She couldn't blame him if housework really wasn't on the top of his list of things to do. Right now his job was to get better. Maybe he could use some help keeping the house shipshape.

When he came back out, she'd managed to finish putting groceries away and tidied the living room. She was fluffing a cushion when his deep voice sounded behind her.

"Don't do that."

She straightened and turned. He'd finished shaving, his freshly bladed face clean and smooth, with only a few telltale blemishes where he'd nicked himself. His eyes were a deep blue, dark enough that the color was nearly indiscernible. As he stood at the gap between the hall and living room, she realized once more how imposing a figure he really was. He was a big man, a man who'd been a soldier since he'd turned nineteen. His raw masculinity did queer things to her insides, and she unconsciously took a step backward. Where had that flare of attraction come from? It certainly didn't make sense. And it was very unwelcome. She definitely couldn't be *interested*.

Besides, she didn't take well to the way he seemed to demand things. As if he were giving an order. She leveled her gaze. "Why not?"

"Because I can do it myself."

She made a wrinkle above her nose. "And you haven't been because?"

That seemed to make him pause. He stared at her and she was determined not to look away. She wasn't used to giving in to intimidation. She never would have lasted through three years of sixteen-year-olds otherwise! She hadn't really considered that teaching high school would be good preparation for dealing with garrulous ex-soldiers. Go figure.

"Because I haven't bothered."

She smiled frostily. "So now you needn't bother. I'm perfectly capable."

He came farther into the room. "Don't you have a job?"

She straightened a throw blanket along the back of the sofa, trying to slow the beating of her heart. Something had happened in the moment when he'd taken a step toward her. Something had passed between his eyes and hers and had set her pulse stammering.

"I'm a home economics teacher at the high school."

He snorted. "You're barely older than they are."

She smoothed a hand over the blanket and

tilted her nose into the air. "I'm twenty-seven, thank you. I've been teaching there for three years."

"So this is how you spend your summer vacation. Charity?" He said it as if it was a dirty word.

"It's hardly charity, Noah." His name sounded foreign on her tongue, as though she shouldn't be using it. What was the other option? Mr. Laramie? Captain? That had been his rank. Neither name seemed to fit the enigmatic stranger before her.

"How much did Andrew pay you to come here today?" His gaze was sharp, pinning her and making a lie impossible.

"Nothing. I did Jen a favor, delivering some groceries and giving you a ride. Although from the looks of this place, it could stand some cleaning up. I could do that, too," she offered.

"What would you charge?"

Charge? Lily stared at him, trying to puzzle him out. The carefree, fun boy Jen had described was nothing like the Noah she was meeting. She wondered if combat had changed him. Or if it was just leaving a piece of himself on the bat-tlefield that had done it. Either way, taking money for a few hours' worth of tidying just felt wrong.

"I wouldn't dream of charging you a penny."

He turned away. "That's charity. I won't have it." He paused, considering, and faced her again. His eyes flickered over the tidy living room and the chaotic kitchen beyond, assessing the mess. "If you were to stay, just for today, I'll write you a check. I am able."

Goodness, Lily knew that. Everyone in Larch Valley knew that Andrew had bought out Noah's half of the ranch. Plus, Noah had been a single officer without a family to support at home. But that was hardly the point.

"Friends help friends," she replied simply.

"Yes, but you are not my friend. You are Jen's friend, and that is different."

She absorbed the snub. It wasn't different, not really. Did he have no concept of doing a favor for a friend? By helping him she was also putting Jen's and Andrew's minds at ease.

And yet, she somehow knew that to say either of those things would cause him to protest further. His pride would demand it.

"If that's the way it must be, then fine." She simply wouldn't cash any check that he wrote.

Besides, it was only this one time. It wasn't as though this would be an ongoing issue.

"Agreed." He gave a sharp nod. "Now, if you'll run me out to Lazy L, seeing as I have no other way of getting there today, that will be the end of it."

She watched with barely concealed curiosity as he went to the door and got his boots, then sat on a nearby stool to put them on. It took him a little longer than it normally would have, but he gripped the pullstrap with his left hand and shoved his foot inside. He did the same with the other foot, and then spent several moments trying to fit his pant leg over top.

She almost offered to help, but if he didn't want her to tidy a cushion, he certainly would take offense to her offer to straighten the hem of his jeans.

"If you're ready," she said quietly.

He stomped out the door without a backward glance. Lily shut the door behind her with a sigh.

She had made a promise to a friend. And she wouldn't go back on it, no matter how stubborn Noah might be.

After she'd dropped him off at Lazy L, Lily went back to the house. He hadn't bothered to lock the door—many people didn't in the small town—and so she went back inside to continue what she'd started while he'd been getting ready.

She ran the sink full of hot, soapy water and began washing the pile of dishes. Jen had called her last night, sounding utterly exhausted, needing to get up at 4 a.m. to be at Snickerdoodles for the day. Lily hadn't thought twice about saying yes to what sounded like a simple request.

Jen had befriended Lily when she'd first come to town, had introduced her around and made her feel that she'd finally found a home. The kind of home she'd never had growing up in Toronto. Home, hah. Home had consisted of a series of apartments, never settling in one place for long. It had meant a new school more years than not, new classmates, new routines. Lily had read *Anne of Green Gables* as a child and had keenly felt Anne's longing for a "bosom friend." But Lily had always been hesitant, knowing that she would end up leaving friends behind when they moved again.

But then she'd come to Larch Valley for her job, and had fallen in love with the town and its people. Jen was the closest thing Lily had ever had to a sister, when it came right down to it. And now Lily was an adult and could make her own choices. And if now and then her town house felt a bit lonely, that was okay. Having a place to belong was enough. And she had a good life. She enjoyed her job. She had friends. She filled her spare time with fun projects.

Not that dealing with Noah Laramie this morning could be classified as fun.

As she wiped a plate and placed it in the cupboard, she decided that the best thing to do was ignore the fact that this person happened to be a very tall, very handsome ex-soldier who'd been a hero on the battlefield. He was the brother of a friend. A cranky, proud brother at that.

Lily worked clear through the afternoon, cleaning the small house until it sparkled, feeling a sense of satisfaction at the shining floors and gleaming appliances. She put some of the chicken breasts she'd brought to marinate. From the look of it, Noah had been eating simple meal-in-a-box type food. A decent dinner would do him good. She was putting together a salad when Andrew's truck drove in the yard, and Noah got out—along with Andrew and Jen. She thought of the chicken on the grill out back. She'd made four breasts so he would have leftovers. Oh, well. At least there was enough if they all stayed for dinner.

Noah stomped inside, using his toes to push off his boots. "You're still here?"

She wiped her hands on a dish towel and opened her mouth to retort when Jen stepped in.

"Noah! What a greeting!"

His gaze skittered away from Lily's as he colored. "Sorry," he murmured. Andrew paid no attention, and Jen blew by through to the kitchen, a parcel in her hands. Lily waited for Noah to look back at her.

When he did, she saw he was embarrassed at the harsh tone he'd used. He shifted his weight on his heels. "I spoke sharply. I just…I figured you'd be finished by now."

"I made you dinner," she said. And yet she was compelled to say more. He had to know this wasn't about the money. "I also made a promise," she said softly, so the others couldn't hear. "And I don't go back on my promises. Not ever." She swallowed, knowing exactly how true that was. Her mind flitted back to the day everything in her life had changed. She had been the one who'd stayed. Who'd waited, hoping. Who had kept her promise. Curtis was the one who had left without a word, breaking her heart in the process.

"Your promise wasn't to me." Noah interrupted her thoughts.

"A promise is a promise just the same."

The words hung for a few moments, until Noah seemed to accept that she meant them. "I didn't know they were both coming," he said gruffly.

"It's your house. You don't need to apologize to me. I was going to leave leftovers for you to have another time, but there's enough food for the three of you. Which reminds me, I need to check on the barbecue."

She disappeared outside, going to flip the chicken and taking a breath, happy to get away from the tense atmosphere that had seemed to envelop her both times she'd been with Noah. For a man in such a predicament, he certainly was independent. He was prepared to fight her every step of the way, it seemed. That was fine. She even admired his tenacity—it spoke of a strength of character. As she turned the chicken over with tongs, she thought of the long days of her summer vacation and wondered how he was going to manage here. There was nothing that said she couldn't help him out while he was away at Lazy L. Cleaning, cooking, sewing… the domestic arena was her specialty. It would give her something to keep busy until school went back in September.

She got the feeling that convincing him would be quite another matter.

When she went back inside, Jen had set the table for four. "Oh," Lily said, surprised. "I'm not staying. You three enjoy."

"But of course you're staying." Jen butted in again, sticking her head in the refrigerator for the salad dressing Lily had brought in with the groceries. She turned around with the bottle in her hand. "We both came because we want to talk to you and Noah about something."

Lily got a strange, dark feeling in the middle of her chest, and she didn't need to look to feel Noah's eyes on her. What on earth could they want to speak to both of them about? Lily swallowed. Today had shown that she and Noah had next to nothing in common.

She got out a plate for the chicken and a bowl for the pilaf that was finishing up on the stove. "And I need to stay for dinner for this?"

Andrew broke in. "Yep, 'fraid so, Lil. You got a corkscrew around here?"

Lily looked at Noah and raised an eyebrow, questioning. Whatever it was, Andrew and Jen were in on it together. Noah seemed to sense it, too, and for a second she felt a brief sense of solidarity with him. Considering their inauspicious beginning today, Lily did not have a good feeling.

"Try the second drawer," Noah suggested, his face unreadable. "If not, I have a multi-tool with one on it somewhere."

She couldn't tell if he wanted her to stay or not. Surely not, after the rude reception she'd received both times he'd found her here. Her earlier thought about helping him more seemed foolish now. She opened the second drawer he'd nodded at and scrounged around, finally finding a corkscrew. She handed it to Andrew, who uncorked a bottle of white wine while Jen took out glasses.

"I recognize these," Noah said suddenly, as Jen handed out the wine.

"They were Mom and Dad's," Andrew answered. He shared a look with Jen and smiled. "When you asked me to find you a place to rent,

Jen thought bringing some things over from the house might make you feel at home."

Noah stared at the wineglass, his lips a thin, inscrutable line.

Jen stepped forward. "We're in the process of combining the two houses anyway, with the wedding coming up."

Again Jen and Andrew shared a look, and Lily got that unsettled feeling in her chest again. It was plain as day Jen and Andrew were ecstatic about their upcoming nuptials, but the mere mention of the word *wedding* made Lily uncomfortable. It brought back so many memories, and none of them good. "Jen, can you put the pilaf in a bowl? I'm going to get the chicken off the grill."

Lily escaped to the backyard, only to realize she'd forgotten the plate for the meat. When she turned around, Noah was behind her, holding it out, a dry, amused smile barely quivering at the edges of his mouth.

"Thank you."

She took the plate and went back to the barbecue. Noah stepped up behind her, and she tried to ignore his presence even though she could feel him there. The air was different somehow.

"They're up to something."

His deep voice came from behind her, and she stifled a shiver that slid deliciously along her spine. "I agree."

"Any idea what that might be?"

Her cheeks flamed, and it had nothing to do with the heat from the barbecue and a lot more to do with the intimate tone of his voice. "No idea," she replied, sounding slightly strangled.

She put the breasts one by one on the plate.

"Hmm," came his voice again, not as harsh but definitely speculative. "Lily Germaine, who seemed completely unflappable to me today, is suddenly put off her stride with wedding talk. Interesting."

She focused on placing the meat on the plate. "Don't be silly." *And don't psychoanalyze me,* she thought.

"I'm many things, Miss Germaine, but silly is one I've yet to be called. I know what a tactical retreat looks like."

She put the cover down on the barbecue and faced him. Granted, wedding talk did tend to put her off the mark. Some disappointments left scars that would never be completely healed. But she'd never say a word to Jen about it. It was her past, her problem, not Jen's. She was happy for her and for Andrew.

"I am thrilled for both of them. They love each other very much."

She went to go by him, but he stopped her with his hand on her arm. "I wasn't talking about them. I was talking about you. I saw the look on your face just now."

Lily looked up, found his eyes serious. As if she were going to tell him anything. If she hadn't breathed a word to her best friend, she certainly wasn't going to spill her guts to some grumpy stranger she'd met less than twelve hours earlier.

"You know as much about me as you need to," she replied carefully, moving away from the warm feel of his hand on her bicep.

"I doubt that," he replied, following her to the back steps.

"And I know next to nothing about you," she said, desperately trying to change the subject. "Besides the fact that you are very grumpy in the morning. Actually, not just the morning, it seems."

They paused, she on the first step and he on the soft grass beneath her, so that their eyes were nearly level. Her heart thumped against her ribs.

"I *am* sorry about today," he said quietly, and Lily knew he was sincere.

"Apology accepted," she breathed. His gaze bored into her and she nibbled on her lower lip.

"The thing is, Lily, I never used to be this moody." Once he admitted it he stepped back, surprise blanking his face. "I don't know why I just said that."

Lily's teeth released her lip and she tried a tentative smile. "Maybe you're trying to make a good impression?"

"I think that ship already sailed."

Then they were smiling at each other. When Lily realized it, and also that they'd been standing there for several seconds, she straightened her shoulders. "We should go in, dinner is ready," she murmured.

Inside, she pasted on a smile for appearances, though Jen's glow eclipsed everyone at the table. Once plates were filled, Andrew lifted his glass, inviting everyone to do the same.

"I want to propose a toast…." He reached out and took Jen's hand in his. "To Jen, for saying yes. To Noah, for coming home. And to Lily, for being her usual generous self."

Lily's smile wobbled just the tiniest bit as they

touched rims and sipped. It was clear that Andrew and Jen were completely happy and it created a bittersweet ache in her chest. Andrew squeezed Jen's hand and grinned. "It's as good a time as any," he said. "We came here tonight to…well, Noah, you're my brother. I came to ask you to be my best man."

"And I want you to be my maid of honor," Jen added, beaming at Lily. They both looked at Noah and Lily expectantly.

Lily gaped; Noah looked down at his plate. After a few seconds of silence, they looked at each other. Best man. Maid of honor. Dresses and tuxes, cake and flowers.

At the thought of having to walk up an aisle in a gown…Lily felt the color drain from her cheeks. She couldn't do it. Even as a brides-maid, she'd be a complete fraud.

At her stunned silence, Jen's face took on a stubborn expression that Lily recognized as her "I'm getting my way" look.

"I…I thought you'd want Lucy." Lily struggled to come up with something to say to cover the confusion in her heart. She hadn't been to a wedding since her own failed attempt. It had been easy to make excuses not to attend over the years. A conflicting schedule, an illness. She had never breathed a word of it to anyone.

But she couldn't make those halfhearted excuses this time. Because right now this wasn't about *Lily*. It was about the best friend she'd ever known, and she felt guilty for hesitating for even a second.

"Lucy is seven months pregnant. Besides, the one I really want is you."

Lily had no response to that. If she were getting married—which she most definitely was not, not now and not in any future she could envision— it would be Jen she'd want beside her.

"Of course I'll do it," Lily replied, reaching over and taking Jen's hand, giving her fingers a squeeze. "I'm honored. You just took me by surprise, that's all." She smiled, feeling as if she was breaking inside. "I've never been a brides-maid before."

"And Noah," Jen went on, her voice soft. "You're Andrew's brother. His flesh and blood. It would mean so much to him. And…to your father, don't you think?"

Lily studied him, saw the battle waging within. He blinked—was that a sheen of moisture in his eyes? She knew he'd never made it back for his father's funeral. Had he even found time to grieve in the midst of all his troubles?

He gave a small cough and acquiesced. "Fine. I'll do it."

"Wonderful!" Jen bubbled over, taking a drink of wine and leaning into Andrew's shoulder. "I told you," she chided her fiancé. Then she beamed at the two of them.

"And, Noah, I'm sure Lily will help you, won't you, Lil? Noah will need a tuxedo." She winked at Noah. "Besides, women do tend to know what needs to be done for weddings."

A lump clogged Lily's throat. Of course she knew what needed to be done. She'd been through it all before. The anguish of seeing Curtis walk away from her before the vows had ever been spoken pierced her heart even now. And Noah…how was he feeling about being asked? He'd only just arrived home from the hospital.

Lily met Noah's despairing gaze, her plans of a relaxing and complication-free school break suddenly out the window. What had they both gotten themselves into?

CHAPTER TWO

WHILE JEN BUBBLED AWAY about the wedding plans and Andrew broke in occasionally with news of the Rescue Ranch, Lily remained very aware of Noah on her right. He said little, instead focusing on his meal and speaking to Andrew about the horses he'd be working with. Lily was wondering if she'd ever get time to catch her breath. All she'd agreed to was delivering a box of groceries, and somehow before the end of the day she was maid of honor and agreeing to guide Noah with his share of best man duties.

"We set a date," Jen announced. "The second weekend in August."

"That's only six weeks away!" Lily put down her fork with a clatter.

Jen poured more wine into Lily's glass before topping up Noah's. "We didn't want to wait. And we wanted to have it before you had to be back at school and, well, at some point Noah will be going back to work, I suppose. And that brings me to the next question. I…I have another favor to ask."

Lily's hand paused on the way to her glass. "Another favor?" She tried hard to keep the hesitation out of her voice. There was no way for Jen to know how difficult Lily would find simply being her maid of honor. The woman was planning her wedding after all. The most important day of a single girl's life. The day that was supposed to come along only once in a lifetime.

"I want you to make my dress, Lily. I don't want some off-the-rack factory dress. I want something that's just me."

Lily's lips fell open. She couldn't stop the rush of emotion at being asked. A woman's wedding dress was the most important article of clothing she would ever wear, and she would only wear it once. Lily's heart was touched by bittersweet emotion. "Oh, Jen."

"I don't know of anyone who could do this any better than you. We can take a day to go to Calgary to shop for materials. It would mean so much."

She could feel Noah's eyes on her, assessing. Lily had made only one other wedding dress before, and it hung in her closet as a white reminder of past mistakes. In one hour she had thought of her failed attempt at matrimony more than she had in the past few years. "Of course I will," she replied quietly. "I'm pleased you would even ask."

As she and Jen chatted about styles and material, Lily could see Noah out of the corner of her eye, providing a welcome distraction. The hinged salad utensils had solved any serving issue earlier, but she was suddenly aware of him struggling to slice into his chicken. He put down his fork and used his knife, but without his other hand, there was nothing to anchor the meat to the plate. Her eyes stung quite unexpectedly. Perhaps he had good reason to be cranky, certainly a better one than she could claim. Life for him was one adjustment after another as an amputee. Even something as simple as eating a meal had its challenges. It was easy to forget that when he was so full of pride and determination.

And she was sure that the last thing he would want was sympathy. What on earth could she possibly say that would help, and not cause embarrassment or humiliation?

She took a breath and turned to face him. "Would you like me to help you with that?"

The table went silent. Lily wished Andrew or

Jen had said something, rather than pretend not to see him struggle. Now they were staring at her as if she'd committed a sin.

Noah picked up his fork and attempted to cut through his chicken with the blunt side of it. But even Lily could tell that the breast was just a little too thick, and that he wasn't as coordinated with his left hand as he would have been with his right. "Noah," she said quietly, all the while feeling Andrew's and Jen's shocked gazes settling on her face. But she focused on Noah.

"I can manage. I am not some two-year-old that needs help cutting his food." There was a hard edge to his voice and it was no less than she expected. And yet to avoid the obvious was wrong, and the only thing she could think of was to be forthright and honest.

"Of course not. And I would imagine you will find it easier when you get a prosthetic. Until then…there is no shame in asking for assistance now and again."

He put down his fork and glared at her. "Again, I don't recall asking for your help."

"You need not ask for it to be offered."

The look he gave her was so complicated she found herself entangled. It was amazement at her persistence and gratitude and anger and annoyance all bound together with a tenuous thread of vulnerability.

He put his fork and knife on the plate and slid it to the side. Without any fuss, she picked up his knife and fork and cut the remainder of his chicken into bite-sized pieces. She laid the utensils back onto his plate and gave it back, picked up her own fork and took a bite of pilaf as if nothing had ever happened. It tasted dry in her mouth, but she was determined not to make a big production out of it.

"Thank you," he said quietly.

The talk around the dinner table resumed, but Lily couldn't get that haunted look in his eyes out of her head.

After dinner Noah and Andrew went into the backyard with coffee while Jen and Lily tidied the kitchen. Lily looked out the window over the sink as she dried a plate. Noah stood an inch or so taller than his brother, his wide back accentuated by the taut fabric of his shirt. A curl went through her stomach when she remembered how he'd looked at her when she had offered him her help.

"Andrew is so glad Noah came home to recuperate," Jen said, taking the dishcloth and wiping off the counter. "We weren't sure he would."

"Why not? This is his home." Lily tore her eyes away from the view and looked at her friend. Jen's lips were unsmiling.

"He's stubborn. At least in that, he and Drew are alike. I think by Drew offering him a temporary job it helped. Noah's so independent, he would hate to be taken care of." Jen put the pilaf pot into the dishwater and turned to Lily. "Thank you for helping today. You really were a lifesaver. Juggling both businesses with wedding plans is proving a challenge."

Lily carefully dried the wineglasses and put them in the cupboard. "Summer holidays are slow. I thought about lending him a hand occasionally."

Jen smiled. "Of course you did."

Lily's nose went up at Jen's knowing tone. "What does that mean?"

"It's what you do, Lily. You make curtains and cook for potlucks and quilt crib sets." Jen smiled. "Lucy told me about the set you did for the baby. You do a wonderful job taking care of people."

Lily tried to accept the remarks as a compliment, instead of with a sting. She had always been that way. There had been times growing up that her little touches were all that made home bearable. Times when it had seemed she was the adult and her mother the child. As a result she'd seemed mature for her age.

"Maybe so," she replied, "but I doubt Noah would cotton to being 'taken care of.'" Lily rested her hip against the counter and twisted the dish towel in her hands. "The only way he would let me straighten up at all was to insist he pay me to do it."

Jen smiled then. "Like I said, stubborn."

Lily regarded her friend with suspicion. "Of course I have no intention of taking his money."

Jen stepped forward and put her hand on Lily's arm, smiling softly. "Of course not. We could have hired a maid for him, or nursing care. He could have hired them himself, if it weren't for his pride getting in the way. But that's not what he needs most, Lily."

Lily's gaze was automatically drawn to the two men again, sipping coffee and talking, though what they were saying wasn't audible in the kitchen.

"I know," she said quietly. She pictured him tugging on his cowboy boots with one hand, so determined to do things on his own. "He needs a friend."

"He couldn't ask for a better friend than you. I know I couldn't."

Lily couldn't resist her friend's heartfelt words, and pushed away the sad feelings that had been resurrected today. She loved Jen like a sister. "Friends I can do. At least you don't have to worry about us dating." She folded the dish towel and put it down on the counter. "Remember, Jen, I don't date cowboys. I should also have said, soldiers." She offered a cheeky smile. When Jen and Andrew had been working through their problems, Lily had made the comment about cowboys glibly and it had become a bit of a running joke between the two friends.

Staring at Noah now, though, she realized she had only been half kidding. There was a certain something about him that caught her attention—and held it. And that would be a mistake.

Jen laughed. "You and Noah? I can't picture it. Two more bullheaded people I've never met. It'd be like mixing oil and water. If I know Noah, this situation is only temporary. Once he gets adjusted, has time to think, he'll be making plans for his future. All I know is we're glad he's here now. Andrew needed the help with the stock and now he gets to have his brother as his best man. And this is a difficult time for Noah. It's fitting that he should be surrounded by family. Right now, we're the only family he has."

Noah said something to Andrew and Andrew laughed, and then Noah joined in. Something warm flooded through Lily at the sound of the laughter. In it was a sense of belonging, of being included.

Lily's gaze once again fixed on Noah's tall profile. Turned this way, his injury wasn't even noticeable. He looked strong, healthy, gorgeous.

She dropped her eyes quickly. No. That didn't matter. Not in the least. Jen was quite right in saying they weren't matched at all. And the last thing Lily was looking for was a boyfriend.

"Anyway," Jen went on, oblivious to the sudden turn in Lily's thoughts, "you handled him just like he needed tonight. He accepted it differently than he would have from me or from his brother. No fuss, no beating around the bush. He'll appreciate your plain speaking, even if he doesn't say it."

Lily took the clean pot and put it in a drawer.

There was plain speaking…and then there were some things that just shouldn't be said at all.

It was only for a few weeks. She could be practical for that long. Absolutely.

Noah grabbed the twine in his gloved hand, heaved and lifted the bale at his side. He staggered a few steps and put it down again with a soft oath and a kick at the golden hay. Sweat trickled down his back. It wasn't so much the weight as the abrupt shift in balance he had to adjust to. He gripped the twine again, and lifted, this time planting his feet wider and distributing his weight more evenly. Once the bale was steady, he headed for the nearest fence in an awkward gait.

Working for Andrew was both a pleasure and a pain, he thought, as he cut the string and folded the knife back up using his thigh and left hand. He distributed the hay to the horses waiting most impatiently for their feed, pausing to rub the nose of a particularly old gelding. Andrew had brought this group nearer the barn for medical attention, rather than letting them graze on the sweeter, green grass of the pasture. Noah admired what his brother was doing, establishing a Rescue Ranch. If he hadn't supported the idea, he might have resisted selling his share to Andrew last year.

But he'd thought he'd be a career soldier. He'd never anticipated being back in Larch Valley again. Certainly not as ranch hand to his younger brother. *Oh, how the mighty have fallen,* he thought bitterly. Not that he held it against Andrew; his brother had been great. But it was a temporary thing, only until he adjusted and got clearance to return to duty. For now it kept him busy and in shape, two things that would speed his recovery.

He reached out and rubbed the nose of the mare, Pixie, one of the thinnest of Andrew's latest rescues. There was definitely something satisfying in having the freedom to work away all day on the ranch, with the sun and the fresh air for company. It provided as much healing as the endless rounds of therapy and doctor's appointments. He hated the poking and prodding, the endless talking about *how* he'd been injured, as if they expected him to fall apart at any moment. Treating him with kid gloves. He shoved another flake of hay into the corral. He'd made a mistake, that was all. As angry as he got sometimes, he thanked God every day that he'd been the one to suffer the consequences. It had been an error but it was his error, and his consequences.

Yet, that wasn't what people saw. Even with Andrew and Jen, everyone saw the injury first, rather than the man.

His mind thought back to Lily and how she'd offered to cut his meat that first night. She certainly hadn't given him the kid-glove treatment. He'd completely surprised himself in the backyard when he'd apologized and then explained about the moodiness. It was more than he'd revealed to anyone.

He didn't know what was in store for him, but he'd spent enough time deployed to know that he had to keep busy and that he'd die being behind a desk somewhere. And yet the army of today tried to keep its soldiers in service. So where did that leave him? He couldn't deny his abilities were compromised due to his handicap.

He shoved the last of the hay into the corral. Handicap, huh. He hated that word. Handicap, cripple, amputee. He'd heard them all and didn't accept any of them. And yet he had no alternative word to describe himself, either.

Most of all he hated needing help. As he

reached the barn, he sighed, absently rubbing the ache in his right bicep, the only part of his limb that remained. Not long ago he'd been a commander of men. From there to needing his chicken cut in pieces. He lashed out and kicked a plastic tub sitting by the tack room door.

"Rough day?" Lily's sweet voice had him spinning around.

"What are you doing here?"

Lily looked pretty again, in a white sundress with some sort of stitching that made her waist look impossibly small. The slim straps on her shoulders set off her golden skin, and the wind ruffled the hem, drawing his attention to her bare legs and feet in intricate little sandals. Her toenails were painted a pastel pink.

"You really do need to work on your welcoming skills."

"You surprised me. Again. You have a habit of doing that, you know."

"No reason to shoot the messenger."

He couldn't help it; he laughed, looking her over with appraising eyes. She was a picture of femininity, and for a few seconds, he'd responded to her as a man would when faced with a beautiful woman. He'd flirted.

Until he saw her eyes shift.

"You wore a T-shirt today."

Her words were soft. Damn, she always spoke what was on her mind, didn't she! And just when he'd been thinking nice thoughts about her practical streak. He refused to look down at the empty place at his side, instead keeping his gaze on hers. She would have seen the stub sooner or later. Might as well be sooner.

"It gets too hot to wear long sleeves."

"And so that is…" She nodded slightly toward his shoulder, where a stretchy fabric covered the end of his arm.

"A stump sock." It was almost a relief to say it. "It protects the sheath, and, well, it looks nicer."

He spoke of his arm as if it were an entity separate from himself, he realized. Well, perhaps it was. It certainly was difficult to equate it with the man he'd been for years. A whole man.

"Does it hurt?"

The straightforward yet gentle question touched him, and he relaxed his shoulders. Lily didn't look away from him, or act strangely. She just said everything plainly, and yet with a compassionate concern that reached in and chased away his resentment.

"Sometimes," he admitted. "I have something that goes over top right now, getting it ready for a prosthetic. And the sock over that. Mostly it's just phantom pain."

She nodded again, her eyes liquid blue as she met his gaze. He couldn't believe he'd actually told her that much. What was it about her that put him off balance, made him tell her things? He'd have to watch that.

"Jen and I went shopping this afternoon. We got the material for her dress."

He blinked as she accepted his answer and changed the subject without offering the sympathetic platitudes he'd grown used to, or further prying. "That's good."

"Yes."

The conversation seemed to lull and Noah found himself gazing into her eyes again. He'd never met a woman as no-nonsense as Lily, and having that trait paired with such femininity was a potent combination. But that was the end of it. Even if he were interested, which he wasn't—*curious* would be a better word—what woman would want a man like him? Maybe *cripple* was a good word. He bore the scars to prove it. More than she knew. He saw the reminders every day when he looked in the mirror.

"I should get back to work."

"Oh…of course." She started to back away, then reconsidered and instead hurried forward, as if afraid she would change her mind. As she looked up at him, he saw a tiny wrinkle form in between her eyebrows and he had the sudden urge to touch it with his fingertip. Oh, Lily Germaine could be a dangerous woman if she wanted to be. It was just as well she was off-limits.

"Noah, wait." Lily stopped only a few feet away from him and looked up into his proud face. Faint freckles hid beneath his deepening tan that came from being in the sun. These past few minutes told her that things were even more awkward between them than before, and if they were going to stand up at the wedding they should at least come to an understanding. Getting through the wedding would be difficult enough without being at odds with him. A tingle went through her, thinking about how they would witness the marriage certificate together, or stand for pictures, or be seated together at the reception. Somehow she felt she needed an ally, rather than a cold stranger at her side.

"What is it?"

"I don't want things to be weird."

He laughed tightly. "Things are already weird. My whole life is different from what I'm used to."

She seized on the opening. "You see? I don't know what that means. And so I don't quite know what to say to you."

"You seem to manage quite well," Noah remarked. His cheekbones became hardened edges and his eyes darkened. "You don't miss a beat when it comes to telling me how it is."

Lily tried not to let the dark expression intimidate her. "You seemed like the kind of man that would appreciate plain speaking."

"I am." He raised an eyebrow, challenging her. "In the army I was also a stickler for insubordination."

She couldn't help it, she laughed. Oh, he could definitely be a piece of work, she thought. He was trying to provoke her. But all his stubborn ways made her far too aware of the breadth of his chest beneath the T-shirt or the way he had tiny tan lines in the wrinkles beside his eyes.

"Do you miss it?" She raised her own eyebrow. "All that bossing people around? It must be very different being here and working for Andrew."

He made an aggravated sound and turned away. She reached out and grabbed his left arm, catching him off guard and spinning him around.

"I'm sorry. That was too much."

He considered her for a moment. "Oh, I was just as used to taking orders as giving them. After all I am only a captain." She was treated to that small glimpse of a smile again. "And Andrew's all right. He made sure I had what I needed before coming back to Canada."

"From Afghanistan?"

He shook his head. "No, Germany. That's where I did most of my recuperating."

"But he didn't go see you, did he?" Lily imagined what it would be like to receive such a call about a family member. Would she run to her mother's side? She rather suspected she would, and for the first time in a long time she wondered about the life Jasmine was living.

Noah pulled away from her arm. "I'm glad he didn't."

Lily gasped. "Why? Surely having your family around you…"

And just like that, Noah's expression closed, as it had the first time they'd met.

"They only send family over if there's a good

chance you won't make it back," he said stiffly. "So I'm glad Andrew never needed to come."

Lily felt very small all of a sudden. There was so much about Noah she didn't know, didn't understand. She wondered how he was making out keeping the house tidy, cooking, all the menial jobs left at the end of the day when he was done at the ranch. She had considered asking him to let her help while she and Jen were doing dishes that first night. Jen had looked exhausted during their excursion today, and Noah needed someone to help. Why not her?

"I'd like to help you, Noah. Even if it's running a vacuum over the floor and taking you to appointments. I know you have appointments, lots of them. And why bother Jen and Andrew when I clearly have the time?"

Noah spun on his heel, striding back to the barn. "I don't need a nursemaid. And my own truck will be here soon."

"Oh, for Pete's sake, I never said a word about nursing!" She scrambled after him, her sandals slapping on the concrete floor of the barn. "Why are you so determined to refuse assistance?"

"Because I need to learn to do it for myself."

"But you don't have to do it all at once, do you?"

He reached for a halter hanging on a hook and a lead, which he looped around his neck. He went back out to the small corral, whistling for Pixie, Lily's sandals sounding behind him. The small bay mare trotted over, and hooking the halter over his wrist he opened the gate and slid into the fenced area with her.

"Can't you find another pet project?"

"I hardly consider you a pet." She couldn't stop the acidic reply and it brought a burst of laughter from his lips. She got the feeling he didn't laugh that often these days. She only wished she didn't feel as though it was at her expense.

She watched, amazed, as he lifted his upper right arm and slid the halter over the stump, and then used his left hand to rub Pixie's head, scratching beneath her forelock. Then he deftly retrieved the halter, slid it up past her nose and over her ears. Once it was secure, he took the lead from around his neck and hooked it on the ring at the bottom.

He led the horse to the gate and with his fingers and hips, maneuvered the gate open and closed again. It had taken him barely a few more seconds than it would have if he'd had two good hands for the task.

"What are teachers making these days? If you need the money…"

Lily's nostrils flared. "It's not about money. I'm fine."

He led the horse back to her, looked down his perfectly straight nose and said, "Then why me? And leave Jen out of it. Even if she is your best friend. Do you feel sorry for me?"

"Oh, please. You make it impossible for *anyone* to be sorry for you."

"Good." With a cluck, he started toward the barn and the veterinary area at the front.

She trotted after him. "Maybe it's my way of saying thank you."

He kept walking. "Thanks for what?"

Oh, he was infuriating! Why couldn't he just accept her help without needing to know the reason? A reason she didn't quite grasp herself. Was he right? Did she need a pet project? She remembered Jen's words—how she was good at looking after everyone. And for one sad moment she considered that Jen might be right.

Doing for others kept her from looking too closely at how lonely her own life was. And damn him for making her remember it. She searched her mind for a plausible reason she could give him. One that perhaps also held some truth.

"For serving your country."

He smiled that tight-lipped smile again. "Right. Well, don't bother. It happens. We were all pinned down during an insurgent attack. I was just the unlucky one that got hit."

That raised more questions than answers, but Lily knew to pry further would get her nowhere. "You don't think what you did was extraordinary?"

He halted, dust rising in puffs from the tracks of his boots. "You know what I think, Lily? I think you're so determined because you're bored. This is farming area. Summer's a crazy time. And here's poor Lily with nothing to do, so she makes wounded Noah Laramie her course for extra credit."

The way he spoke made her blood boil, partly because of the insolence behind it and partly because she already knew it was just a little bit true.

"You want to know the one thing I learned when I moved to Larch Valley? People help each other. It was an amazing concept to learn. When someone needs a hand, it's there. How on earth do you think your brother got the Rescue Ranch started? I helped Jen then, too, and with renovating the bakery. Now if it makes you feel better to pay me, by all means. I certainly wouldn't want to wound your male pride."

Noah started walking again, the horse trudging along behind, unconcerned with the arguing going on. "Ouch."

"It's more than that, Noah. Has it occurred to you that you need to get fitted for a tuxedo? Shoes? That you have duties as a best man? What about a bachelor party? Have you thought about that?"

She stood back with a satisfied smile at the blank expression on his face. "Ah, so you haven't. Tell me, do I strike you as the kind of woman who wants her escort to show up in jeans and boots?"

His nostrils started to flare. Well, good. Noah was pretty transparent, whether he thought so or not, and she seemed to get her own way best when she stood up to him. "Moreover, do you think Jen and Andrew want that, either?"

"Andrew said he's just pleased I'm home to see it."

"Yes, and Jen is planning her wedding. Her one-and-only wedding, Noah. Do you know what a wedding means to a woman?"

"Everything."

Her stomach quivered. "Yes, everything," she breathed, remembering the dress hanging in her closet. She'd never had the heart to get rid of it. "A woman wants her wedding day to be her fairy tale. All her dreams come true." She wanted to help give that to Jen. The kind of wedding that Lily had never had. One with a happy ending. Proof that it could happen.

"Is that why you didn't say more at dinner the other night?" He angled his head, looking at her curiously. "Because I saw your reaction when the wedding talk started, remember? Why is that?"

Lily squinted against the sun as she looked up at him. How did the conversation suddenly get turned around so that the spotlight was on her? "Jen is my friend. I would do anything for her. Even stand here and argue with your stubborn head. I consider it part of my maid of honor duties."

"I warn you, Lily. I'm not pleasant to be around."

"Tell me something I don't already know," she challenged.

"I mean it, Lily."

"So do I." She reached out and put her hand

on his left forearm as the lead rope trailed out of his palm. "I am their friend, and you are their family. Doesn't it make sense that we should try to be friends, too?"

Once she said it she knew it made the most sense of any argument she'd put forth. "Friends" was safe, wasn't it? The skin beneath her fingers was warm and firm and she looked up. Her gaze caught on his mouth, the finely shaped lips with the perfect dip in the centre.

He said nothing, and her breaths grew faster, more shallow as the moment held in the hot summer afternoon.

Pixie got tired of standing around and nudged Noah with her nose, sending him off balance and forward. Lily's hand gripped his forearm and her other reached for his T-shirt as their bodies bumped together.

Her breasts were flattened against his rib cage and she felt the quick rise and fall of his breath. His deep-set eyes looked into hers, wide and with an awareness that hadn't been there before. For a second it almost seemed he leaned closer, but then she blinked and his jaw tightened as he stepped back, steadying her on her feet with his hand and tightening his grip on the lead.

"Friends," he stated, though she detected a sliver of skepticism in his tone. "We'll see, Lily. We'll see."

He walked away, Pixie trailing behind, leaving Lily with nothing to do but watch his retreat.

CHAPTER THREE

LILY PICKED UP NOAH in her compact car. When he came out of the house, he had a small bag over his shoulder and sunglasses shaded his eyes. His jeans were neat but well faded and broken in, the way a good pair of jeans was meant to be. Despite the heat, he wore a long-sleeved tee in brown, the right sleeve pinned up to cover the stump sock.

Lily briefly remembered being breathless, pressed up against his chest. It was just as well they only had the wedding and summer vacation when they'd be seeing each other on a regular basis. After that, she'd be back teaching. And she'd be focused on what she needed to be focused on. Work. Routine. And who knew what was in store for him?

"Thanks for the lift this morning." He opened the door and slid in, only to find his knees pressed against the dash.

Lily laughed at the comical sight of his legs folded up in the small space. "My lord, you're a giant for this little car. Handle's in the middle, between your legs."

He reached for the lever, heaving a sigh of relief when the seat slid back and he could extend his legs a little bit. He put his bag on the floor between his knees. "It isn't quite a Humvee, is it."

He seemed in better humor this morning, despite the day they had ahead of them. "It suits my needs," Lily replied lightly. "It's practical and economical."

He twisted, reaching across with his left arm to grab the door handle and slam it shut. It took him two tries and a low grumble to get it latched so that the little red dash light went out. His good mood seemed to dissipate as he slid his glasses onto the top of his head. "And you are a practical woman, aren't you."

She prided herself on her practical streak, and yet the way he said it felt like a criticism, not a compliment. He reached across himself once more and grabbed his seat belt, crossing it over his middle and fastening it. She put the car in gear and started out the drive, heading toward

Main Avenue and from there to the highway to take them north. She felt his eyes on her and returned the look when they stopped at a stop sign. She forced a smile. "I try to be."

"It is an unexpected trait," he mused, shifting and settling into the upholstery. "You're so..." But he broke off, turning his head to look out the window.

"I'm so what?" Her heart tripped a little bit. It shouldn't really matter what Noah thought of her, but somehow it did. Maybe because, even though she'd known him such a short time, she already had a sense of his strength and honor. Even his bouts of grumpiness were understandable under the circumstances. She realized she didn't truly care if he *liked* her, but it was important that he *respect* her.

"Never mind."

"No, I want to hear it. I'm so?" She did want to know what he thought. She'd spent a long time in her mother's shadow, and people expected her to follow in her mother's footsteps. Jasmine Germaine always seemed ethereal. Beautiful, wispy, moving with the breeze. She had never seen the need for roots the way Lily had. She'd moved them more times than Lily cared to count when she'd been a child, all the while insisting something bright and shiny was around the corner. All Lily had wanted was some stability. To have the same bedroom more than a year at a time. Time to be a kid.

It had been her mother who had been popular, and loved, a beautiful and fragile butterfly with a handsome man on her arm. Lily had always faded into the woodwork when Jasmine was around.

"I was just going to say…"

She noticed a few spots of color on his neck. Was he embarrassed, for heaven's sake?

He cleared his throat. "You're very pretty, Lily. Your name suits you."

She stared out at the highway as heat flooded her cheeks. Noah thought she was pretty?

But she wasn't the pretty one. That was her mother. Lily was the practical, steady one.

"My compliment doesn't please you."

She kept her eyes on the road. "I'm just not used to anyone calling me pretty, that's all."

She could feel his gaze on her and she was resolved not to look away from the pavement.

"What do they call you, Lily?"

She took a breath and remembered what Jen

had said at dinner. That she looked after people. "They call me handy to have around."

Noah's rusty-sounding laugh filled the car. "Well, you are that."

His deep chuckle wrapped around her. Was he flirting? A lightness filled her body, something that felt an awful lot like happiness. Was Noah Laramie actually capable of flirting?

"So which do you prefer, Noah? The pretty or the practical?"

Dear Lord, she'd gone and flirted back! What was wrong with her? When he was around she seemed to forget her common sense.

The air in the car grew heavy as the question settled. The smile slid from Noah's lips. "I didn't think the two had to be mutually exclusive. And what difference does it make which I prefer?"

"It doesn't," she answered quickly, but the words came out clipped. It couldn't make a difference. They were just friends for the time being. She certainly wasn't fishing for more.

But Noah's gaze bored into her, seeing far too much. She felt him shift in his seat so he was partially facing her. "It's perfectly allowable to be both, you know. There's nothing wrong with it."

The breath she'd been holding came out in a

wisp and she tried to smile. She didn't want to be judged on her looks, yet knowing he found her attractive sent an expansive warmth through her. "Thank you, then, for the compliment."

They drove on for a few minutes more before his voice broke the silence again.

"Lily?"

"Hmm?"

"What do you want me to see when I look at you?"

Her hands grew slippery on the steering wheel. What did she want from Noah? The answer came back swiftly: nothing. She did not want to get personally involved with him. Friendship was far enough. She thought he was a good person in a difficult situation. But anything more...not again. She'd keep her life ordered and complication free, thank you.

"Your future sister-in-law's best friend," she replied, reaching over and turning up the radio.

She heard him chuckle beside her, and it made her curious. "What?"

He leaned his head back against the back of the seat and closed his eyes. "If nothing else, you keep things interesting."

The weight that had seemed to hover over the

conversation dissipated like a fine mist. She couldn't help the smile that curved her lips in response. "Is that a good thing?"

"Very good. I tend to live in my own head a lot. You help me stop doing that when you're around."

"What kind of things do you think about?" All the headlines lately seemed to talk about returning soldiers and post-traumatic stress. Surely losing an arm in a firefight was grounds for some serious trauma. She found herself wondering what things he suffered that she knew nothing about.

"Oh, you know. What to have for breakfast. What shirt to wear."

"In other words, none of my business." She glued her eyes to the highway, put on her blinker and passed a transport truck as they climbed a hill.

He still had his eyes closed as he answered. "Stuff that talking won't solve," he said, his voice low.

She risked a glance and saw he still had his eyes closed. "Are you tired?"

Noah nodded, just a little, opening one eye to squint at her. "A little. I didn't sleep much last night."

"How come?"

"In my own head again."

She had wondered if his arm pained him frequently, but instead now pictured him lying awake thinking. Wondering if he dreaded his doctor's appointments. Wondering if it was memories of combat that kept him up while the rest of Larch Valley slept.

Wondering if he'd been thinking about her the way he seemed to sneak into her thoughts lately.

"Are you worried about today?"

He shrugged, and she spared another glance sideways, seeing how his eyelashes lay against his tanned cheeks. "What's in the bag?"

"Mostly paperwork. The army's part of the government. There are forms about forms and so on."

"About your discharge?"

"So many questions today," he replied drily, opening his eyes.

"We're going a hundred and ten on the highway. Not like you can get away, is it."

That at last got a smile from him. "I can always refuse to answer."

"But you won't because…"

She was teasing, but when she turned her head

at his prolonged silence the mood quieted to nearly somber. She could see the deep blue of his irises and the black pupils within them. Her face heated as she forced her attention back to the road where it belonged.

"I'll be damned if I know, Lily. I haven't spoken to anyone about this unless I was ordered to."

She wasn't sure how to feel about being his confidante, and yet she wanted to know the real Noah. "Maybe it's easier because you don't really know me," she suggested.

"Maybe," he agreed. He leaned his head back against the headrest again. "Anyway, I'm not discharged. I'm what they call a temporary category."

She hadn't considered he was still truly in the army. She'd never seen so much as a uniform around his house. "It sounds like they don't know what to do with you."

He chuckled. "Maybe not. The idea isn't so much to know where I'll end up, but to give me the time to get there, I suppose. Then figure out where I'll be sent to next. Right now I'm being paid to get better." He frowned. "It feels ridiculous."

"Why?" She kept her eyes on the road, but she could sense his frustration anyway. "You were hurt doing your job, and it's only right you don't suffer financially while you recover, right?"

"I guess."

"So the agenda today is…?"

"Following up with the doc, talking to a head shrinker, and physio."

Lily couldn't help it; she laughed at the matter-of-fact way he put it. "Psych follow-ups, you mean."

"Yes. In case there's mental and emotional trauma after the fact. And believe me, it's far nicer when you get debriefed when you're healthy. It's a vacation. I missed out on that part when I was in Landstuhl."

She swallowed. It was different hearing him verbalize the possibility of PTSD. He'd admitted to internalizing things too much. The Noah she'd seen so far seemed unlikely to have such problems. But maybe he was just good at hiding them. Maybe her impressions were completely off base.

It wouldn't be the first time she'd misjudged someone's character. Curtis had turned out to be a very different person than she had hoped. Not nearly as strong as she'd thought, for one.

Not nearly as committed, either.

She pushed back the painful memory and

focused on the present. She was also helping Noah get fitted for his tuxedo today. "I think you're more likely to be traumatized by what comes *after* your appointments today."

"I think you might be right," he agreed, sliding down in the seat a little more so his knees were nearly against the dash, and closing his eyes once more.

A few moments later she looked over and his lips had fallen open, relaxed in sleep.

She had to be very, very careful. Because she was starting to like Noah Laramie. Too much.

Lily read a book and drank coffee while she spent the day in waiting rooms outside the physio clinic, the psychiatrist's office, at the pharmacy, and at the Area Support Unit while Noah paid a visit with paperwork in hand. It was midafternoon before they left the Currie Barracks and made their way to Macleod Trail to the formal wear boutique. Noah was already looking tired from his day of poking and prodding.

"We can do this another day."

Noah sighed and shoved his pack into the backseat. "That means another trip to town and prolonging another physio day. I'd rather just get it done. Besides if we don't, the first thing Jen will do is remind us how few days there are until the wedding."

Lily shut the car door and led the way to the store. "You're probably right. I'll try to make it painless."

Inside they were greeted by a pleasant salesman who took one look at Noah's arm and then raised his gaze politely to Noah's face.

"We're here to rent a tuxedo," Lily explained, as Noah stared around him at suits, shoes and novelties.

"Is the wedding party registered here?"

"No…the groom has his own tux. We'll only be needing the one."

"Sir?"

Noah turned from looking at the silver flasks at the counter and straightened at the word *Sir*. Lily had the sudden thought that perhaps he missed that particular word. It was as indicative of his former life as the uniform, she would imagine. She wondered why he wasn't wearing his dress uniform for the wedding. She hadn't even thought to ask. She wondered if it was his decision or Andrew's request.

"May I take your measurements, sir?"

Noah and Lily followed the salesman to a back portion of the store, where the clerk retrieved a form and a measuring tape. After filling out the information, he procured his tape. But as he began to stretch it out, Lily saw him hesitate next to Noah's arm. His cheeks suddenly colored and he stepped back.

"I'm…I'm sorry, sir." He stammered and then cleared his throat. "I don't know if you're comfortable with…I mean I…"

Noah's eyes darkened. "You mean *you're* not comfortable."

Lily sensed the impending storm. Noah had had people poking and analyzing and asking questions all day. Getting fitted for his tuxedo was definitely not a good idea. He was tired and she felt the frustration coming from him.

The clerk swallowed and bravely met Noah's gaze. "I simply don't want to presume, or inadvertently hurt you."

"Noah." She stepped in front of him and caught his gaze, hoping to send a well-meaning caution. "I think he's just unsure. It's awkward, that's all."

"Dammit, Lily," he warned in a low whisper. "I didn't want to do this in the first place."

"Then why not wear your dress uniform?"

For a moment Noah's gaze held hers. "Because for this one day I am not Captain Laramie. I am the brother of the groom."

"May I proceed, sir?"

A muscle in Noah's jaw ticked. Lily thought maybe everyone would be more comfortable if she used the tape measure. The clerk could note the measurements, and Noah might lose some of his stoic resentment.

"I'll do it," she said, loud enough that the attendant could hear. "Or we'll do it together." She lowered her voice, put her fingers over Noah's. "Is that okay? Someone needs to measure you."

She saw him swallow. Other than the afternoon when they'd been pressed together, they had avoided touching. Suddenly her great idea seemed intensely intimate, and her tongue slipped out to wet her lips.

"Fine, you do it," he said sharply, his gaze dropping to where the tip of her tongue had disappeared back into her mouth.

Lily took the tape from the attendant and smiled. "I do a fair bit of sewing." It was an understatement, but right now she just wanted to keep everyone happy. "Just tell me if the line isn't exactly where you want it."

Her fingertips grazed the muscles of Noah's shoulders as the tape stretched across the breadth of him. She measured down his left arm, meeting his eyes only briefly when she murmured words about using the same length for the right—it would be pinned up out of the way anyway. She heard him catch his breath as she wrapped the tape around his slim waist, and she had to remind him to relax and let the breath out. The fabric of his shirt was soft and warm against her fingers, and butterflies tumbled in her stomach as her hands rested against the button of his jeans for a few breathless moments.

This wasn't what she'd had planned when she'd told herself she was going to keep Noah at arm's length. The way she was responding, and the way he was holding himself so rigidly, told her an arm's length away was still too close.

"I need to do your chest," she said quietly, and she reached around him. She guided the tape measure beneath his arms, her fingers touching his right bicep lightly as she adjusted the tape. Did it hurt? Did it feel odd to move that part of his arm without the rest of it attached? His heart pounded against her hand as she brought the ends of the tape together. Touching him this way made her too self-conscious to ask. She read out the measurement instead and the man put it on his clipboard.

"Now there's just the inseam," he chirped, oblivious to the tug-of-war going on between Lily and Noah. "You should have on proper shoes to measure that," he explained. "You're what, an eleven?"

Noah nodded. As the salesman scurried away to retrieve dress shoes, Noah's voice came from above, deep and husky. "Lily…"

"There's a chair over there. Why don't you sit to change your footwear," she blurted, more affected than she wanted to admit by the rough way he'd said her name. She did not want to be the pretty girl who'd lent a hand. Someone who had his attention now, when he needed her, but would one day be forgotten. It was better to keep it strictly platonic.

Noah hesitated the smallest instant, and for a minute she was afraid he was going to say something more. But he went and sat and pushed off one boot with his toes. The second required more pushing, and she gave in and knelt before him, gripping the heel and sliding it off his foot.

"I hate this," he admitted in a low voice. Lily's eyes stung. Grouchy Noah was a challenge, but a Noah who had started to trust her was far more difficult to handle. In only a short week he'd started accepting little bits of help, like the drive today to his appointments. She almost preferred the stubborn, irascible man to this one. It was easier to keep her distance from him. Easier to keep her thoughts in line with where they should be.

The salesman arrived with a shoe box. Lily took the shoes, unlaced them, and put them on the floor for Noah to put on his feet while she talked to the salesman about what style tuxedo they wanted to coordinate with Andrew's. She wouldn't do everything for him.

When she turned back, Noah's cheeks were red. He had the toe of his right shoe holding down the right hand lace of the left shoe, while he tried to negotiate the other tie into a semblance of knot and bow with one hand.

"Dammit!" he finally exploded, sitting back on the bench and closing his eyes while his jaw trembled with frustration.

"Could you give us a moment?" Lily asked the salesman in a whisper. When he'd discreetly left, she went to Noah and sat on the bench beside him.

"Noah—" she began, but he cut her off.

"Don't," he commanded, and she recoiled from the venom in his voice. "Don't you dare try to placate me or say it's understandable or whatever it is you are going to say. I can't stand it."

All the platitudes she'd had on the tip of her tongue, the ones about needing time to adjust and how things would get better and it was understandable to be frustrated fled, driven away by the force of his words.

"All right."

For several minutes she waited, feeling the vibrations of resentment lengthen and weaken. He finally reached over and took her hand. "I'm sorry."

"You have nothing to be sorry for." Relieved, she turned on the bench so that her knees touched his. "You are allowed to feel the way you feel."

"Helpless? Is it okay for me to feel helpless?"

"How can I answer that without saying any of the things you've forbidden me to say?"

That drew a reluctant smile from his lips. "Touché."

"Look, we're almost done. Why don't you just let me tie them this once."

"Because I need to do it myself."

"Why?"

His eyes glittered at her, angry and resentful. "Because I do, okay?"

"Does this have to do with your wounded male pride?" She tried to lighten the mood but he didn't smile. Oh, no, a smile would have been preferable to the searing gaze he treated her to. There was an intensity to Noah she couldn't deny, and it drew her to him no matter how many times she told herself it wasn't smart.

"Yes," he said simply.

Something sizzled in the air between them. Lily looked away first. "We can argue about this later. Right now the salesman is wondering what the heck is going on. Will you let me tie them, please?"

He nodded, and she squatted down, deftly tying the laces while he clenched his jaw tightly and stared past her to the change rooms, his gaze closed off and unreceptive.

Every one of his struggles seemed to hit her square in the heart. He was so proud. She knew he hated it every time he attempted something and failed. His occupational therapy would teach him tricks to manage everyday tasks, she was sure. He just wasn't there yet.

Lily beckoned the salesman over again and took the tape measure in hand once more as Noah stood up, shaking down his pant legs. Suddenly she seemed to realize exactly where she was measuring—his inseam. Embarrassed, she couldn't find it within herself to meet his gaze. She tried a smile on the sales assistant, knowing it was futile to think he didn't sense her discomfort. "I think you can do this one?" she suggested.

The man took the tape back and deftly made the measurement. Lily couldn't help it, she finally risked a look at Noah, and her lips quivered as he waggled his eyebrows at her. He knew. He knew why she'd suggested the salesman take the measurement and he was teasing. Her heartbeat took a little lift. After his outburst, a sense of humor was like a ray of sunshine.

"Fantastic," the clerk said, beaming. "Let's try on some styles to be sure, shall we? The four-button notch is a great choice. What colors for the vest and tie?"

"Just white," Lily replied when Noah shrugged. "This is why you needed me with you," she chided, offering a small smile. "You wouldn't have had a clue on your own."

"Hey, I've had my wardrobe supplied for the last few years," he replied. They could see the clerk hovering at a rack, fiddling with hangers but obviously listening in. Noah leaned forward and said in a stage whisper, "That happens in prison."

Lily gaped and fought hard not to laugh. She turned her forehead to Noah's chest, hiding as soon as she saw the clerk's eyes widen. Inaudible giggles shook her chest as she felt his smile next to her temple. His joke took her so much by surprise she had no opportunity to guard against it.

"Oh, come on, you know now he's wondering what I was in for and how I lost my arm," he murmured, his breath warm in her ear.

"You're terrible."

The smile faded; she could feel it as the warmth at her temple disappeared. "It's been a rough day. I don't want to lose my temper again. I'm sorry, Lily, for being so short with you. For allowing myself to get frustrated. It's just safer to have fun with it. Maybe I need to start laughing more."

While they were waiting, Lily leaned back. "Does this feel like a prison now? Being ripped out of the life you knew?" She searched his eyes, marveling at how the layers of Noah seemed to be getting unwrapped today—both good and bad.

"Sometimes. When I get frustrated, like I was with the shoes. Or when I just miss the life. I thought I was a career soldier. It's tough to be a civilian after this long."

"Ah, here we go. Four-button notch with a white vest and tie." The clerk put the clothing on a hook in a dressing room.

Noah reached for the safety pin holding his sleeve, but he couldn't seem to get it to release properly. After a half-dozen tries and a healthy sigh, he turned back.

This time she didn't ask. He was tired and his patience was at the breaking point. He needed to get this over with and get out of here.

She reached for the pin, odd circles of nerves twirling around her insides as she touched his stump for the first time through the sleeve. It felt like any ordinary arm, only it was wrapped beneath the shirt and ended above the elbow. She wasn't sure what she'd expected. Something harder, less pliant perhaps. She was careful, not knowing if it was still tender to the touch.

"The wedding is in August. I think we'd better plan on pinning you twice. Once with the jacket for the ceremony, and then with the jacket off for the reception due to the heat. I can help you with that. I'm a whiz with pins and things. No one will even be able to see it."

She clipped the safety pin closed and smiled up at him, the edges of her lips trembling.

"You don't need to."

"As maid of honor, I consider it one of my duties."

"No, what I mean is that I'll be able to do it myself."

Lily frowned. Despite needing her help today, he wasn't showing any signs of letting up. In the meantime, he was frustrating himself to death.

"I'll be out in a few minutes."

He took the clothes into the change room while Lily and the clerk waited. The clerk had said very little since Noah's surprise revelation.

It took slightly longer than it would have normally, but Noah finally stepped out from behind the door and Lily caught her breath.

He was stunning. His eyes gleamed above the

fine lines of his cheekbones, his dark hair
mussed slightly from pulling his T-shirt over his
head. His tan set off the snowy white of the shirt,
which he'd buttoned to the second top button.
The vest lay taut against his flat stomach, and the
jacket was unbuttoned. The shirt was tucked
rather unevenly into the trousers. All in all, he
looked like a man at the end of the day rather
than the beginning, and it was arresting.

"The tie," she said, reaching forward and buttoning the top button. "We won't get the full
effect without the tie."

The skin of his neck was warm against her
fingers, and she fought the feeling that this
whole afternoon was something a girlfriend or
wife should be doing, not a recent acquaintance
or sudden bridesmaid. He swallowed and his
Adam's apple bobbed against her fingertips. She
slid the silk tie around his neck and fumbled her
way through a Windsor knot, remembering quite
painfully performing the same task for a very
young, very fresh-faced groom. Lord, she'd been
so young, and so naive, so sure everything was
going to work out the way they'd planned. She
saw the empty sleeve at Noah's side in her
peripheral vision. Surely Noah had had dreams

of his own. How many had been quashed by the loss of his arm?

"Andrew will help you on the day. I'm afraid I have had less experience with ties than safety pins."

He couldn't look down with her hands holding his chin up, and she noticed the smooth line of his jaw. There were no missed shaving spots today.

Lily then put her hands on his lapels and drew the jacket closed, buttoning up the four buttons. Andrew had said his tuxedo was similar, and she knew the two of them would look handsome standing at the altar together.

At the altar. Lily's hands grew cold at the thought. Everywhere she turned lately there seemed to be a reminder, making her relive her failures over and over again. Perhaps it was good that there wasn't much time before Jen's big day. It would be over and Lily could go back to the business of forgetting.

She stood back, assessing his appearance. The sleeve would be tucked up neatly on the day. And she'd walk up the aisle in the pale pink dress she'd already started cutting and pinning.

At the front, she would move to the left, beside

Jen. She'd never be caught as the one in the white dress. It wasn't that she was against marriage. Not at all. She'd just already learned it wasn't for her. Not everyone was as lucky as Andrew and Jen.

"You look very handsome," she said dutifully, as the assistant picked and pulled at the coat a few different ways, making alteration notes.

"Even if it's not my dress uniform?"

Lily stepped back, putting distance between them. She almost wished he was wearing it, if that would make him seem more of a stranger. She had to ignore the physical attraction that had woven its spell this afternoon. That was all it was. Attraction. Perhaps a smidgen of curiosity. Nothing more.

"You can take the man out of the uniform, but not the uniform out of the man, I see."

"Being out of it was not my choice." He reached for the dressing room doorknob and then looked over his shoulder. "None of this was my choice, Lily. My mistake, maybe, but not my choice. Don't forget that."

Lily stared at the closed door for a few moments. What could he possibly mean, his mistake? And it felt very clear that he wasn't just talking about his injury but the current situation, which included her. She wanted to feel relieved at the stinging rejection. Starting something with Noah was not on her agenda.

But it stung just the same, and she retrieved her purse from the floor to hide just how much.

CHAPTER FOUR

NOAH DISAPPEARED BACK INTO the dressing room to change again. He spent a frustrating few minutes putting the pin back in his sleeve, cursing under his breath as the pin sprung open and dropped to the carpeted floor. He didn't have to do it himself. He could have asked Lily and she would have performed the task in an instant.

But she'd done enough for one day.

When he stepped out of the change room, he was completely buttoned and snapped. Lily rose from the bench and came to him, her lips curved up in a reassuring smile. He'd felt so helpless, so…impotent…when he'd needed her help with the shoes. It was demoralizing when you were trying to impress a woman. And he was trying to impress her, he realized. He wasn't sure how or why her opinion had started to matter, but it did.

"If I could just get you to sign here, sir, and

pay for the deposit," came the clerk's voice from behind them. He was still holding the clipboard.

Noah reluctantly broke eye contact with Lily and followed the clerk to the reception area where he dug out a credit card for the rental deposit. He'd probably been too harsh earlier, speaking to the salesman. But he wasn't used to the stares yet, or the way someone's eyes automatically darted to his empty sleeve first and then to his face. He wasn't used to looking completely inept in public, either, or losing his cool.

And he wasn't used to the way Lily had looked at him, and touched him. The gentleness of her fingers, the way the feel of them against him made him feel more of a man than he had in many weeks. Which was foolish. She didn't want him. They were merely thrown together. The last thing she'd want was a man with his scars. The touch on his stump today was as close as she was going to get to seeing his wounds. He didn't want the ugliness of war to touch her the way it had him.

And yet he found himself telling her things he couldn't bring himself to say to Andrew, or even to his army buddies when he one-finger typed e-mails to them.

He took the pen in his left hand and painstakingly signed his name to the document and credit card slip. He scowled at the uneven letters that looked the equivalent of a child's scrawl. Learning to write with his opposite hand was yet another one of his challenges.

The clerk stared at the card and then the signature and paused. Noah stiffened, but was determined to hang on to his temper. He knew the clerk was only doing his job, comparing signatures. "I used to be right-handed. I'm having to relearn to write with my opposite hand."

The clerk flushed deeply. "I'm sorry...I mean...I didn't realize. I'm required to match the signatures...."

Lily put her hand on Noah's arm. The gesture was reassuring and he exhaled. He couldn't fault the man for sticking to his orders, even if it was an inconvenience to him. "It's okay. I know you're just following procedure."

Lily spoke up, squeezing Noah's wrist. "If you like, I'll give you my credit card number."

"No, this will be fine," the clerk assured

them. He lifted his chin. "There won't be a problem, sir."

Noah pocketed his wallet again and they left. Once they got into her car, he let out a gigantic sigh.

"I'm so sorry, Noah. For all of it."

"This is why I hate going out. I spent my entire day either being stared at or poked. I should be able to sign my own damn name! A five-year-old could do better."

"Give it time. I'm sure the occupational therapy will help."

Noah let out a bitter laugh. "Do I strike you as a patient man, Lily?"

"Not particularly."

He turned his head to look at her. Lily put the car in gear and headed out toward Highway 22. "Do you want to stop for dinner on the way back? We haven't really eaten all day."

"If I have to see one more person today…"

Lily spluttered out a laugh. The aggravated tone reminded her of the old *Honeymooners* reruns her Gram had watched on the television. But she understood his need for quiet. She couldn't blame him for not wanting to spend any more of his day in public. She suddenly wondered if part of his reluctance to be in the wedding had to do with feeling on display. She certainly felt that way, and she had nothing as gossipworthy as a war injury to contend with.

"Fair enough. No restaurant then." But it was going to be early evening before they got back. She couldn't just drop him home. The only thing they'd had during the day was a coffee at a drive-through.

"Why don't you let me cook you dinner?"

They were stopped at a light and she looked over. His jaw was so firm, so defiant. He needed to relax, needed a night away from Lazy L and doctors and reminders.

"At my house. You haven't seen my house yet. I have lots of groceries and a bottle of wine I've been saving for when I had company."

He raised an eyebrow and her lips twitched. "Sue me," she said carelessly. "I don't usually sip alone."

"That actually sounds good."

"Then it's a date."

At Noah's shocked expression she back-pedaled. "Well, obviously not a real date…"

Silence fell in the vehicle once more as the

light changed. As they accelerated down the highway, Lily wondered how much deeper she was going to let herself get in before she started bailing out.

Noah's first reaction to Lily's house was surprise. She unlocked the front door to the stuccoed duplex and they stepped inside. It smelled of vanilla and something lightly floral. The small foyer was painted a warm, welcoming yellow. As he followed her past the stairs and to the kitchen, he was surprised at her color choices. The same yellow was repeated on the walls there, with splashes of chocolate and terracotta lending a cozy feel. The colors were repeated on pottery canisters, and a tall potted orange tree sat in a corner by a south window. He smiled. If the landscape was slightly different, he'd almost feel he was in a hacienda rather than a duplex in suburbia.

"Make yourself at home," she said, putting down her purse.

To the right was a living room, and the colors there picked up the red tones. Caramel furniture and cherrywood floors mellowed the deep shade of the walls. He wandered to the doorway and stared at a painting on the wall. It was a cacophony of flowers in yellows, reds, purples, so vivid the blossoms almost seemed to jump out at him.

"Is there something wrong?"

He turned around, looking at Lily standing in jeans and a plain pale blue T-shirt, holding a bottle of wine in her hands. "It's just that this wasn't what I pictured your place to be like."

He'd come to somewhat accept her help. Dinner for two at her house wasn't really in the plans. But the thought of going out somewhere to be gawked at again had been unbearable. It had seemed like a good solution at the time.

Right up until the moment she'd made a point of insisting it wasn't a date. As if he needed a reminder. He was starting to realize she was a dynamic, competent woman. And today he'd demonstrated how he could neither tie his shoes nor write his name. Not exactly date material.

"What did you expect?" She went to work on the cork, and he saw the way her shoulders curved as she manipulated the corkscrew. Her dark hair lay over one shoulder and he had a momentary urge to go over and push it aside, so that it cascaded down her back. But after this afternoon, that was a very bad idea. He took a step backward and put his hand in his pocket.

"I expected lighter colors. Pinks and blues, maybe."

"I like earth tones," she responded, finally getting the cork out and retrieving two glasses. "They make me feel warm and comfortable and content."

"It's a very nice house."

"It's not very big, but there's just me."

And now tonight he was there. He wondered how much socializing Lily did and if she had teacher friends. If she entertained, if she dated. He accepted a glass of wine, murmuring his thanks and taking a small sip. It occurred to him that while she had been given a crash course in Noah Laramie, he knew next to nothing about her.

It also occurred to him that he wanted to know more. Maybe it was his military background, but he liked to get a complete picture about who he was dealing with. It made for a more level playing field. Lily knew far more about him than he was comfortable with, while she was surrounded by secrets. Surely he could find something to fault. It would make it easier not to like her quite so much.

He walked to the door that opened to the small back deck. "What brought you to Larch Valley in the first place?"

Lily took a bag of tomatoes out of the fridge and lined them up on a cutting board. "Work. I had my degree but no job. LVHS was looking and I applied. It's a lot easier to find a job out of province."

"But so far from home…you're from back East, right?"

Her knife paused for a moment. He wondered why the slight hesitation and watched as the blade moved again, finely chopping the red flesh of the tomato. "Yes. Ontario."

"What about your family?"

The knife rested on the cutting board then as Lily looked up. "Is this the interrogation equivalent of *get to know you better?*"

He grinned then, knowing he'd inadvertently struck a nerve. He'd gotten the impression that Lily had few faults beyond her stubborn nature. But there was something here. And it felt wonderful to turn the spotlight on someone else for a change. He got tired of being the focus of scrutiny.

"Sorry. Occupational hazard. I was feeling a little at a disadvantage. Not really fair for you to see all my dirty laundry now, is it."

A reluctant smile tugged at her lips. "I suppose not. But my life really isn't very interesting."

He left the view from the door behind and went to stand near her at the center island, watching as she heated olive oil and garlic in a pan and added the tomatoes. "No one grew up in a bubble," he said simply. "Fess up."

She sighed, stirring the mixture with a wooden spoon. "My mom still lives in Toronto. There was only ever the two of us, at least after my Gram died when I was small."

"Does she visit here a lot?"

A dry laugh greeted his question. "No, she's never been here. We sort of keep our lives… separate."

Lily focused on the bubbling tomatoes rather than on Noah. Wasn't he just full of inquiries today. Innocent questions, too. Only they weren't that innocent at all. The last thing she wanted to do was get into the complicated relationship she had with her mother. Or why they didn't see eye to eye on almost anything. They'd stopped talking mostly, just to avoid arguing.

Noah put his hand over hers on the spoon. "I haven't seen my mom since I was seven."

His fingers were warm and slightly rough and felt good on the smooth skin just behind her wrist. "I know." She thought of the young boy he must have been, left with his father and a baby brother. At least Lily had grown up with a mother, for all her faults.

Still, she appreciated the confidence, and the fact that he'd shared a tiny bit of information about his childhood. His hand slid off her wrist and she avoided his eyes, instead reaching for a bunch of fresh basil and chopping it for the sauce.

"I'm sorry about your dad, too." She scraped the basil into the sauce and put the cutting board down on the counter. "I know you didn't make it home for the funeral."

Noah's face twisted and she felt guilty for causing him more pain. "Oh, Noah, I'm sorry. I didn't think it would make you feel worse."

Noah shook his head. "In some ways I'm just glad he doesn't have to see me like this."

"Noah!" Dismayed, she forgot her earlier promise to keep the evening nontactile, and she reached out, gripping his forearm in her fingers.

"Surely you don't think he would care about your injury. That it would make a difference."

His gaze met hers. "I don't know. He always seemed so proud that I was a soldier. Said that if I wouldn't be a rancher, this was the next best thing. Somehow I can't escape the feeling that I failed him. It made going to his grave pretty difficult."

"But you did go."

He nodded. "Andrew drove me when I first got back. It was my duty to go. Andrew's made his peace. I don't think I have yet."

"A parent loves their child, no matter what the disappointments. And I can't imagine your father was disappointed in you. He must have been very proud." She squeezed his arm and smiled.

And yet she knew there was a false note to her words. Jasmine had never accepted Lily's version of life. She'd accused her of limiting her options. While the words had never been said, Lily knew her mother was disappointed in her choices.

"That was a very nice diversion, Lily, but we were talking about you." Noah slid his arm out from beneath her touch and grabbed the wooden spoon, taking a turn at stirring the sauce. "So a job brought you to the Larch. What made you stay?"

"I've made my home here," she said finally. "I love Larch Valley, I love my job, and I've made friends. What more could I ask for?" She stopped short of saying it was the kind of home she'd always wanted. There was stability and order and a routine that was comforting. She'd never liked living life on a whim. She liked going to the grocery store and knowing the cashier by name. She enjoyed seeing the neighborhood kids grow and change. And knowing she had people like Jen and Andrew and the Hamiltons as a surrogate family was a blessing.

"It's a good place to call home," he agreed.

Lily watched him wander through her kitchen and bit down on her lip. It was silly that she should be feeling drawn to him in any way. Their lives were drastically different. But the things that made up Noah were hard to resist, and each time she saw him face a new challenge she felt connected to him a little more. He was strong and brave and a little bit angry. And his motives seemed to have very little to do with her, which was a refreshing development. It was clear he wasn't interested in her romantically. The look on his face when she'd said the word *date* had spoken volumes. She'd had to hastily backtrack before he started thinking she did have a thing for him.

Lily shook her head slightly. She should be relieved. After all, if he wasn't interested in her, then it was only herself she had to worry about.

She put water on for pasta and took a sip of her wine, wanting to change the subject. The past was where it should be—behind her. It was better to talk about the future. "What are your plans for after the wedding?"

He frowned, the scowl marring the handsome perfection she'd glimpsed when his face was relaxed and smiling.

"I don't know. I suppose I'll start talking to someone about new positions and postings. At some point I have to get back to work, and the sooner the better."

Lily let out a slow breath. Why was she worried? This was nothing more than an itty-bitty attraction. A few months and Noah would be gone again anyway. He certainly wasn't looking for a relationship. And neither was she. Knowing he would be putting his uniform back on and heading to a new base made him just a little bit safer.

"Your condition won't make a difference, then?"

"It all depends on my rehab and doctor's orders. Who knows what limitations they'll put on me. But they try to keep people who've been injured in the service these days. They'll rustle something up. I've got rank and experience going for me."

She dropped her shoulders and made her hands busy stirring the sauce. That was it then. He wouldn't be staying. Any elemental attraction of the moment on her part wouldn't be a concern. So why couldn't they make standing up for Andrew and Jen fun, instead of a chore?

Why couldn't they just clear the air and get it over with? Why not just tell him why she was dreading it so much?

But the words refused to come as she slid spaghetti into the boiling water and went to the cupboard for pasta bowls.

"Well, that's good then. At least you can reclaim something of your old life, right? A few months and you could be back in uniform and captain again. That must make you happy."

"Sure."

Yet as he said it, she saw a shadow lurking behind his eyes, and she got the feeling the sentiment came laden with conditions.

"And we might as well make the best of this wedding business, don't you think? I mean, you're only here a short time, and I'm not looking for anything romantic, so why don't we just agree to keep it light? We might as well have fun."

Yet, even as she said it, she kept feeling the way his chest had been wide and strong beneath her hands this afternoon, the way she'd had to damp her lips with her tongue as he'd come out of the dressing room with the tux on. Just who was she trying to convince here? Many more scenes like that and he *would* start thinking she had designs on him.

He stepped forward, putting his glass down on the countertop. Lily's heartbeat seemed to pause for a millisecond before starting up again slightly faster than before. He was only a breath away from her, and her hands itched to reach out and draw him closer. She didn't want entanglements. But she did want *him*. Not that she'd admit it in a million years.

"You don't strike me as a keep-it-light kind of

woman," he said softly, his deep voice penetrating right to her core.

"Oh, but I am." She panicked, scuttling away as the pasta threatened to boil over, knowing it had been many years since she'd allowed herself to "keep it" anything. "I definitely choose *keep it light* over *hot and heavy.*"

She turned her back to him, attending to dinner, but the way her senses were clamoring around, she knew *hot and heavy* was exactly what had been running through her mind.

Lily carefully took the cardboard box out of the backseat of her car and shut the door with her hip. Andrew's truck was gone and so was Jen's car. She'd just leave the supplies and head back home. She could do with a day to tidy up her own place and possibly even spend an hour or two on the deck with the latest paperback she'd picked up at the drugstore.

The door to the house was open and she stepped inside, marveling at the transformation since Jen and Andrew had gotten engaged. Gone was the plainness that she'd seen during her first visit. There was fresh paint on the kitchen walls, and the yellow and white accents were brought out even more by Jen's subtle touches. Lily went through to the living room and put the box down on the sofa. Inside, Jen would find the stationery she had ordered as well as the materials to put together table centerpieces of floating candles and silk flower petals. She reached out and grazed a finger over a cool glass bowl. There'd been nothing like this at *her* wedding. It had been rushed and simple and…

Footsteps clumping up the porch steps pulled her out of her thoughts. As the front door slammed open, she pressed a hand to her chest before rushing to the kitchen to see what the commotion was about.

Noah was at the sink, water rushing into the stainless steel basin as he added soap to the water. "Dammit, dammit, dammit," she heard him mutter.

"Noah?"

He spun, water flying everywhere, his face blank with shock at having her appear before him. He turned back and shut off the water. "Give me a hand here," he commanded, and she immediately went forward.

"Did you hurt yourself?" For a moment she

felt a shaft of panic that he might have done something to his one good arm.

"No. Beautiful's foaling and Andrew's in Calgary with Jen. I can do it but…" He shoved his hand in the sink and swished it around. "This is stupid. I need to scrub up and I obviously can't scrub my own arm."

Relief rushed through her as she stepped forward. "I'll do it for you." She grabbed the antiseptic soap and began working his fingers through her own. "Why didn't you use the sink in the barn?"

His voice came from above as she worked the soap with the spray from the tap. "The faucet broke yesterday and we didn't get a chance to fix it yet." He chuckled as she continued, her fingers working in a most businesslike fashion, the warm sound doing swirly things to her insides.

"Lily?"

"Hmm?"

"You need to go up past my elbow."

She blanched a little. A farm girl she was not, but she dutifully scrubbed and cleansed until she dared any germ to get in her path.

"There," she breathed once she was done. Even a job as brusque and businesslike as washing his hand seemed intimate these days. In fact, since their meal the other night, she'd barely been able to think of anything else.

"Thanks. Now I'm going to need your help."

"My…my help?" She stammered the words out, her fanciful thoughts scattering. Washing hands was one thing, but she'd never birthed anything in her entire life. Nor had she had any burning desire to. "Noah, I don't know…."

He looked down at her, so solid and confident she felt like ten times a heel.

"Beautiful will do the work herself. I'm just there for backup. But I don't even have a full set of hands, Lily. If I need something, it would be helpful for you to be there to hand it to me."

She nodded mutely, staring down at her jeans and white sneakers. What in the world was she getting herself into?

She trotted after him to the barn, his long strides eating up the ground between the two buildings. As they neared the door, he offered her an encouraging smile. "Relax, Lil. Keep your voice soothing and soft—it'll be comforting. Imagine you were having a baby and how you'd like it…no bright lights, no loud noises, just soothing and comfortable, right?"

Lily blinked back stinging tears and squared her shoulders. He couldn't know how his words hurt. Maybe it was the renewed experience of being involved with a wedding or the fact that every time she saw Lucy and Brody together she was reminded. She'd thought she'd done a good job of forgetting and moving on. But lately it seemed to hit her from every corner. Once upon a time she had wanted children for herself. She and Curtis had talked about it, agreeing to wait until after they were finished school and both working before starting a family. A girl and a boy. Lily held back a sigh. Once upon a time she'd dreamed of a happily ever after that didn't exist. A happy ending that she was no closer to now than she was before.

But if Noah was willing to do this one-handed, she could find the wherewithal to help.

They stepped inside the dark barn, quiet except for some shuffling from the stall nearest Andrew's clinic space. Noah grabbed a box and slid inside the stall, simply watching as the mare lay on the bed of soft straw.

"Shouldn't we do something?"

"Not yet. Hopefully we won't have to." He

spoke in a low voice. "I can't believe Andrew's not here. We knew it would be soon, but we kind of expected a late night, not a midmorning birthing."

Lily looked around her. The mare lay on her side, breathing heavily, the whites of her eyes showing. The straw was dark beneath her and Lily got a horrible feeling.

"Noah…" She stared pointedly at the spot, but he only smiled.

"Her water broke, just like a woman's would. That's all."

"You've clearly done this before." Maybe he didn't need her help and she could escape to the house.

"I grew up here. Of course I did, many times." He smiled at her, and it seemed to light up the dim stall. "Some of my favorite memories are of the three of us down here late at night when a mare was foaling. Afterward Dad always made us hot chocolate. Sometimes, if it had been a very long night, we got to miss the morning of school."

"He indulged you."

Noah nodded. "Not often, but sometimes." He kept a close eye on the mare. "This time I thought we'd have the resident vet in attendance. We don't know much about her history, previous foals, nothing. Jen basically rescued her from the side of the road."

Lily was familiar with the story, and the fact that Noah's agitation had subsided helped to calm her, as well. Her eyes widened as one hoof emerged, then another. She held her breath as she waited.

After several minutes without progression, Lily saw Noah's brow pucker. "Hand me the towel," he said softly, and Lily bent to retrieve the soft cotton from the kit. She watched, fascinated, as Noah crooned low words to the horse, amazed as he used the stump end of his right arm to anchor the towel against the tiny hooves as he wrapped it around and then gripped the fabric in his large hand.

"What are you doing?"

"Giving her a little help."

Mesmerized, Lily watched as Noah worked on his knees, easing the hooves toward the mare's feet rather than out, inch by inch. "Good girl," he murmured, sweat beading on his forehead. Lily saw his bicep bulge as he tugged gently but firmly.

The head and shoulders appeared and Lily gaped, unable to turn away from the beautiful sight. For a few moments mother and foal rested, and then it was over. Head, shoulders and hind-quarters, with only the tips of the foal's feet left to come.

"Hello, gorgeous," he murmured warmly, running his hand over the foal's head. "Look at you." He sat back on his heels. "What a girl. Barely needed a bit of help."

"Why aren't they moving?"

He smiled up at her, a big celebratory smile that took her breath from her lungs. "They're resting, see? And in a moment she'll be up and then I'll need your help for just a few moments more."

"You didn't need my help at all." She stood by the stall door, only a few feet away, but she could feel the relief and joy emanating from him.

"I might have, though. A little pull is nothing. You never know if there are going to be compli-cations. I'm glad you were here."

Suddenly Lily was, too. She'd seen a side of Noah that was beautiful. Capable and strong, but gentle, calm and affectionate. She smiled as the mare struggled to rise and the umbilical cord broke.

"A clean break. Fantastic. Can you hand me the iodine? It's just there." He pointed.

She opened it and watched as he gently doctored the umbilical stump.

"Great…look at that. Mom and baby and all's right with the world."

The last word faded away slightly, and Lily caught a glimpse of telltale moisture in his eyes. She rushed forward, looking up at him, searching for signs of pain. What if he'd overdone it? She was pretty sure foaling wasn't on his list of physio activities. "Noah? Are you okay? Did you strain something?"

He shook his head, moving past her. He grabbed the kit in his hand and led the way out of the stall. "No. I just realized I've missed this."

She trailed after him. "The farm?"

"I'm usually in the middle of places where *nothing* is right with the world, you know? That's why I'm there. To try to fix it."

There were times she had paused to wonder about his past, about what he'd seen in his years as a soldier. If his experience had affected him in the ways she read about in the paper or saw on the news. The thought that he might have to suffer through that as well as his physical injury made the July day suddenly seem cold. "Do you have nightmares or anything?"

He shook his head. "No, nothing like that, thank God. It's just a whole other world from here, and I think I got used to it. Numb. But in some ways those are lost years. I lost touch with Andrew. And with my father. When I found out he was sick there wasn't any way I could come home. Now it's too late."

"I'm sorry about Gerald."

"Nothing we can do about it now. Sometimes all you can do is move forward." He clenched his jaw after he said the words, and she wondered what he was remembering.

He walked to the barn door and she followed, turning her head to stare at the stall again. "Should we leave them?"

"I'm just going to wash up again and come back. There will be more to do in the next few hours, but nothing I can't handle until Andrew returns."

In the kitchen once more, Lily put on a pot of coffee and made Noah a sandwich. She put it before him and stood back, letting her hand rest on his shoulder briefly.

He crossed his left hand over and covered hers,

the contact searing her skin. There was something here, something begun much earlier. For a second she considered removing her hand from beneath his, but then she remembered the look of happiness on his face as the foal had been born, and she found she could not pull away.

He pushed his chair back and her heart jumped.

He stood, holding her fingers still within his as he faced her. For long, quiet seconds he gazed into her eyes, the deep-set blue pulling her in. He pressed the palm of his hand flush against hers, then twined their fingers together.

"Noah," she breathed, a warning lost in a sigh.

He took the last step forward and dipped his head, touching her lips with his own.

CHAPTER FIVE

NOAH'S LIPS WERE WARM and rich from the heat of his body and the taste of the coffee. With a sigh, Lily melted against him, feeling his wide chest against her breasts as she lifted her face to him, curling her hand around the nape of his neck while her other hand remained entwined with his.

He moved their joined hands so that they were pressed against the small of her back, pushing her closer into his body, and the kiss deepened. It had been a long time, too long, she realized, since she'd kissed a man. Since she'd wanted to. Her lashes fluttered as he murmured against her lips and her hand slipped down over his shoulder, avoiding his partial arm and sliding over his ribs instead.

When they broke off the kiss, Lily stepped back, even though what she really wanted was to curl up inside his embrace and feel cherished there.

That in itself was reason enough to back away.

"We shouldn't have done that," Lily blurted out as Noah's keen eyes pinned her to the spot. With a breath of panic, she realized that with a slight movement he could have her close again.

"That bad, huh."

Bad? She studied his face but he didn't look as though he was joking. It hadn't been bad in any way, shape or form. It had been fantastic. That was why it was a mistake. But she knew admitting it would be an even bigger error in judgment, so she stayed silent.

"I beg your pardon." The air between them seemed to turn quite chilly now. His lips became a thin, inaccessible line. "I overstepped. It was an interesting morning."

Damn, now she'd gone and offended him. That hadn't been her intention. "There is no need to beg my pardon." She tried to smooth it over by offering a conciliatory smile. "We both know there can be nothing between us, right? It just happened. That's all. As you said—it's been an interesting morning."

Interesting wasn't the half of it. She'd seen a side of him that was unexpected; gentle, quiet, tender even, as he helped bring the foal into the world. She was usually immune to that kind of sentimentality, instead choosing to see the big picture. And the big picture here was that Noah was at an in-between place in his life and would be leaving as soon as he was able. If she kept on, she would be a casualty. She must be losing her edge.

Noah sighed, turning away and going to the sink for a glass of water. "Seeing the mare and foal…it reminded me of what it was like to be home before. When times were simpler. Sometimes it feels so strange, being here, being in this kitchen." He drank deeply of the water and put the glass on the counter.

"You've been gone a long time. Maybe too long."

He nodded. "Yes, in some ways, the army became my home."

A home away from here, Lily reminded herself. A home he wanted to return to. She was realizing it more every day. It had been foolish to give in to the kiss. Keeping it light was how it had to be. *This time* she had her eyes wide-open, and he would be leaving. She had to keep herself from caring. And sneaking kisses didn't help with that objective at all! She needed to find a way to put some distance between them.

Noah rested his hips against the counter and

stared toward the hallway that led to the stairs. "I haven't even been through my things, do you know that? I've stayed in the rented house, been here for a few meals at Jen's nagging."

Her insides seized as he talked about being home; he couldn't know how the truth of his words resonated within her. Home was something she hadn't had, not really. Not with a deep history like Noah's. For a moment she forgot about the kiss and the upcoming wedding and how she needed to keep her distance while at the same time keeping things amicable. No, he'd touched a nerve. Here he had a perfectly fine home—where he was wanted and welcomed and he seemed to be turning his back on it when he should need it the most.

"Perhaps you should go up. This is your home. I don't know why you'd feel odd coming back to it. I'll bet there are all kinds of things left up there."

Lily went to the far counter, tidying up the sandwich fixings while Noah studied her with sharp eyes. She couldn't meet his gaze. Did he realize how much he was taking for granted?

"I'm not the same boy who left."

"So what? It doesn't change who you were, or

the fact that that boy was the reason you became the man you are now. It doesn't change that Andrew is your brother. Or that he worked very hard to make sure you came home to get well. It means a lot to him that you're here. Maybe more than you realize."

"So you think I'm ungrateful?" He pushed away from the counter.

Did she? Lily pondered that for a moment. "Not ungrateful, exactly," she amended. "I think you have tunnel vision right now. It's understandable. A lot has happened to you."

He looked down at his arm. "You think?"

Lily knew that whatever she'd gone through was nothing compared to Noah, and it had left invisible scars as well as the obvious. He had a lot to work through. But it bothered her that he suddenly seemed to be taking Andrew and Lazy L for granted. He had sold out his share. Andrew had brought Noah home because that was what real families did.

"What I think is I need to get going and you need to check on Beautiful and her baby. And then I think you need to spend some time reacquainting yourself with Noah Laramie. Your room would be a good start."

"And I suppose you want to help me with this, too."

Lily grabbed the cold cuts and put them back in the fridge, keeping her hot cheeks away from Noah's astute eyes. She was already in too deep simply by caring. By going now, she would be away from the temptation of kissing him again. "You've fought my help since the beginning," she pointed out, turning from the fridge and leveling him with a stern look. "This time I agree with you—I think this is something you need to do on your own."

"Right."

He went to the door and out onto the veranda. "Where are you going?" she called after him.

"To check on the mare, like you said."

Lily picked up her purse and stared after his retreating figure. He was angry, and a part of her felt badly for being blunt. But another part of her wondered if any of what she'd said had penetrated his thick skull…and if it might make a difference.

Andrew had taken over with Beautiful and the new filly the moment he'd arrived back at Lazy L. When Jen had asked about naming her,

Andrew had given her an indulgent smile and a knowing look at Noah. "Women, they have to name everything like it's a pet."

But Noah had interrupted, remembering the look of awe on Lily's face as the foal had been born and his first words to the latest addition to the Lazy L herd.

"Gorgeous," he said. "Her name is Gorgeous."

Andrew had laughed and Jen had been delighted.

But now they'd gone out to the barn together and Noah was left in the farmhouse all alone.

Maybe Lily was right after all. Maybe he did need to remember the boy he'd been. It was as if there was a distinct line in his life. One side said *before the army* and the other said *in the army*. But where was he now? Certainly not out, but not in, either. And there had been some good times here. Good times like the ones he'd re-membered today.

He took the stairs slowly, wandering up to his old room. The door was ajar, and he pushed it the rest of the way open, flicking on the light switch. The window blind was down, and he crossed the room to open the slats, letting in summer evening light. He turned the light back off and stared around him. Nothing had changed.

Nothing. It remained exactly as it had been when he was nineteen and heading to boot camp. For a few years he'd returned during his leaves, but Andrew and his father always seemed to be at odds and it hadn't been enjoyable. And since then, he'd barely been home for visits, and then only short ones. He hadn't been home in five years. And now he regretted it.

The navy comforter was unmussed on the bed, the shelf on the wall still contained his softball and hockey trophies. On the scarred pine dresser was the framed photo of his graduation from boot camp. Another of the day he'd become an officer. It was clear Andrew hadn't touched a solitary thing in here. Nor had Gerald. What had they been waiting for? The boy he'd been wasn't the man who had returned. Seeing his things waiting for him should have been comforting, but instead it made Noah feel even more like a stranger. What had happened to that young, idealistic boy? Where had he finally left him behind? Afghanistan? Bosnia?

The truth was that the house at Lazy L didn't actually feel like home anymore. He felt more relaxed, more contented, in the little rented house closer to town. Today as they had watched

Beautiful's foal being born...that had been the first time that he'd really felt things click into place. He'd missed things about being on the farm. He'd remembered some happy moments when it had been the three of them all together.

Lily had been with him. And he'd been a fool and kissed her.

Noah sat heavily on the bed, hearing the box spring creak under his weight. He had let her simple touch carry him away, and then he'd slipped completely under her spell the moment her lips touched his. He'd been wanting to do it ever since the day he'd tried on the tux and her arms had come around his chest.

And practical, pretty Lily had been darkly sweet. He hadn't anticipated the punch to the gut response. Noah ran his hand through his hair, frowning. And then what? Even if he wanted to take it further—which he had, at least at the moment—he couldn't. He couldn't let her see him the way he was now. He couldn't bear to see her soft smile turn to horror, and that's what would happen if she saw what war had done to him. An army life was no life for her, but it wouldn't matter because as soon as she saw the marks it would be over. He could learn to rewrite his name, he could learn to tie his shoes and drive a car again. But he couldn't take the scars away. He couldn't change a single, damn thing.

His jaw hardened and he got up from the bed. One kiss and here he was, thinking about her and reminiscing in his old bedroom. What good would it do to remember? Not a bit that he could see. When he'd said that the boy he'd been was gone, he'd meant it.

He shut the door behind him with a firm click. When he'd said kissing her was a mistake, he'd meant that, too.

But then he leaned against the door frame, closing his eyes. Somehow he had to find a way to keep his attraction to her at bay. No more moments of weakness. The wedding was coming up, and for the sake of peace he would somehow manage to keep things amiable between them. He enjoyed her company. There was no reason to make the wedding a tense affair. He'd lock up whatever feelings he seemed to be developing, because no good could come of it. And when the wedding was over, he'd see about his options for the future.

Back in the part of his life that made sense.

"Noah."

He opened his eyes, startled by the sound of his brother's voice saying his name. He turned his head, saw Andrew at the bottom of the stairs. "Hey."

"What are you doing up there?"

Noah schooled his features. He didn't want Andrew to know how he was feeling about the house or about Lily. Lily was their friend. And Lazy L… It was clear to Noah that Andrew was really proud of what he was doing. Lily's words still rang in his ears. Andrew had wanted Noah to come home. If Andrew was trying to make up for lost time, he was too late. Their father was gone. The years were gone. What they had to work with was *right now.* And as much as he had no desire to hurt his brother, he couldn't look too far into the future yet. It was simply too big, too daunting.

"Just checking out my old room."

Andrew nodded. "You got a minute for a walk? I want to talk to you about something."

"Sure."

Noah looked at his bedroom door once more before going down the stairs. He pulled on his boots while Andrew waited on the porch, and then went outside. Wordlessly they started walking, heading toward the west hay field.

The sun was still in the sky but its light had mellowed as summer suns do. The blades of grass held a rosy hue, and the scattering of clouds across the sky had pink and lavender underbellies. It was Noah's favorite time, when there was slow warmth and the day was gently sighing that the work was done. At this time of day sometimes it was hard to believe he'd ever left.

"I'm glad you were here today," Andrew began. They slowed their steps, stopping before the boundary of the field, watching the grasses wave in the wind. "I didn't expect the mare to deliver."

Noah thought back to how relieved he'd been to see Lily in the house. It had been a long time since he'd helped a mare foal and he'd been afraid. Doubted that he could have handled any complications with one arm. But Lily had been there, backing him up, and he'd felt strong and capable when she'd beamed as the foal stood for the first time on wobbly legs. He swallowed hard. "I was glad to do it."

"You've been more help than you know, Noah. This summer would have been impossible without you being here."

"You would have hired someone."

"It's not the same as family."

Noah got an uncomfortable feeling in the center of his chest. Andrew hadn't looked at him while he was speaking, instead staring off into the distance. He didn't want to disappoint Andrew. It had been good, connecting with him again. But if Andrew was hoping for more…

The uneasiness grew as neither said anything for a few minutes. Finally Noah broke the silence, nodding at the hay field. "Just about time for the second cutting, don't you think?"

Andrew nodded. "Dawson said he'd do it. Look, I asked you out here because I have something to tell you."

And he didn't sound the least bit happy about it, Noah realized. Was it Jen? The ranch? Noah? "Just come out with it then." He hooked his thumb in his front pocket and faced his brother square on. A clean cut healed best.

Andrew met Noah's gaze and admitted, "I invited our mother to the wedding."

Noah's breath came out with a whoosh. "What? Our mother? Do you even know where she is?" He hadn't seen his mother since he was seven years old. He'd seen his father's heartbreak after she'd abandoned them, had seen how

Andrew had been so confused and had kept waiting for her to come home. At seven, he had understood certain things slightly better than his little brother. But she hadn't ever come back and he'd never gone looking.

"She's been in Grande Prairie all along. I've seen her. Twice."

"But for the wedding…" Noah understood this was a big deal for Andrew. He even understood that Andrew wanted their mother there. Jen's parents would be there. It was a natural time to want family to be together. But they weren't a real family. It had all the potential of a big disaster. Maybe he wasn't well versed on other best-man duties, but this was one time he felt up to the job. And right now that was delivering a heavy dose of realism.

"Are you sure that's a good idea? I know you want her there, but think about it, Andrew. She hasn't been back in Larch Valley since she walked away from it. Memories are long here. You know that."

"Of course I do. Believe me. It wasn't exactly a picnic when I came back, you know. And there's always the chance she won't come. But she's the only family we've got, Noah. How can I not ask?"

"It's your wedding, and your decision," Noah replied.

"What about you, though? Noah, you've just come home. I don't want to upset you."

"And you haven't. Surprised, yes. But to me, she is a stranger. I accepted it a long time ago. She didn't seem to care about family all the years she was gone. I don't expect any of that has changed. It's one day. If it's what you want, I'll manage."

Andrew sighed. "There's more, something I should have told you long ago but didn't know how."

"More?" He let out a harsh laugh. He thought of standing up with Lily at the wedding, knowing how beautiful she was going to look and how he kept trying to hide his scars from her. Now there appeared to be family drama added to the mix.

"Gerald was not my biological father."

Nothing Andrew could have said would have surprised Noah more. Gerald had raised them both. "What are you talking about? Of course he was."

But Andrew shook his head. "No, he wasn't. And he was the one that made Mom leave. She was having an affair when I was conceived. But when she did it again, it meant the end of the marriage. And he refused to let her split us up. She left rather than face a big custody battle."

"And this is supposed to make me feel better?" Anger rushed through his veins, revitalizing him after the initial shock. "The fact that we're now half brothers?"

"Is that what bothers you? Not the affairs?" Andrew's words were laced with incredulity.

"I knew about the affairs. For the most part anyway. I heard more of the arguments than you did." Noah's anger had flashed and was now fading away. "And you're my brother, no matter what. What makes me mad is that you kept it from me."

He took several steps away, needing to walk, to expend some of the emotion bundling up inside him. Was *nothing* in his world staying the same? Through it all, he'd held on to Lazy L and the presence of his brother for stability while the rest of his world changed. Now that seemed to be slipping through his fingers, too.

And when Andrew had come asking to buy him out, he'd said nothing.

For the first time in days he almost felt the presence of his right arm even though it no longer existed. He could feel his hand balling into a fist, the cording of muscle as he longed to punch something in anger. But the bone and muscle and flesh were gone. Never in his whole life had he felt so impotent.

He stopped, hung his head and fought to calm his breaths, trying to make the sensation go away. "You should have told me."

"I don't expect you to understand it all in an evening. God knows I didn't," Andrew said quietly, coming to his brother's side. "And I knew about the parentage thing since before I left for university."

"That long." He couldn't keep the bitterness from his voice.

"It was what caused the rift between Dad and me. I wish I'd had the chance to make peace with him when he was alive. He was a good father."

Noah swore softly. "I had no idea. I really didn't."

Andrew put his hand on Noah's shoulder. "Our mother loved Dad in her way. She knew we'd have a better life with him than we would with her."

"You've had more time to think about it than I have."

"I know. I didn't tell you before because I was still trying to make sense of it myself."

The firm hand slid off Noah's shoulder and Andrew took a step back.

"Noah?"

"Yuh."

"This doesn't change that you are my brother. In every way. Remember that."

Noah heard Andrew's boots scuff away in the grass, but he stood a long while, looking out over the waving hay field. He'd only just started feeling that he was getting his life back. And now he felt more alone than ever.

CHAPTER SIX

THE PUNCH BOWL HELD the remnants of a pink punch, the soda pop in it now flat and tasteless. Pink, lavender and white bows topped a paper plate hat trimmed with ribbons, and plates and pastry crumbs were scattered over the pink tablecloth. It was the remnants of a frilly, girlie bridal shower. As maid of honor, it had been Lily's duty to host. And it had been fun.

Hostess duties had kept her occupied over the afternoon, but now, looking at the mess left behind, Lily couldn't stop the sadness that crept into her heart. She had never had a shower. Planning to run away had meant that no one was supposed to know. There had been no silly games, no punch, no bows and cards and presents to unwrap. There'd been no bachelor party for Curtis, either. This afternoon Noah had taken Andrew, Dawson and Clay golfing in lieu of a stag party. It was all so very traditional. Predictable.

Thinking about it wore her out, and Lily simply didn't have the heart or ambition to clean everything up now. She turned her back on the messy kitchen and headed for the stairs. She had to keep her hands busy with something else. The wedding was only days away and she still couldn't seem to get the waist right on Jen's dress. She could work on that instead, and later, when the echoes of laughter and well-wishing had faded, she'd put her house to rights.

Upstairs, Lily slipped the dress over her hips and reached behind her, pulling up the zipper. She studied the mirror, tugging gently at the strapless bodice. Her figure wasn't a match to Jen's, so the fit wasn't quite right, but she could tell if there were puckers or pulls where there shouldn't be. The organza overskirt was being particularly fussy to work with and she was struggling with the waistline. She smoothed and tucked with her fingers, frowning in the mirror. It should have been Jen trying it on now, but she and her mother had taken her shower gifts back to her house. Lily frowned, working with the fabric, trying to see where the adjustment should be made. She wanted it perfect for tomorrow when Jen came to do the final fitting.

She sighed, knowing that this wasn't quite breaking her promise to herself. After all, if she'd had a dressmaker's dummy, the dress would be on it now instead of her. When she'd vowed she'd never put on a wedding dress again, this wasn't exactly what she'd had in mind. And she supposed it had been a rash pronouncement, one made in anger and mostly out of hurt and disillusionment.

If she'd really meant it, she would have thrown away the dress. The one that still hung in her closet. The one with the chiffon overskirt that had taken days to get just right…

She stared at the closed closet door for a long moment, then unzipped the zipper of Jen's gown and hung it on its special hanger. She put it in the closet and her hand rested on a white opaque bag. She'd managed to keep the overskirt flat and flowing just right in the end. If she could only see it on… Once again she wished for the dummy to help solve her problems. Her brow puckered. Did she dare? Even thinking about putting it on felt like tempting fate.

She remembered that day so clearly. The rush for the flight, the excitement of checking into the hotel room and the surreal moment of putting on her wedding gown. The moment of sadness as she missed having someone to help her with her hair, her crystal necklace that she'd made herself. Then the sadness giving way to excitement when Curtis had knocked on the door.

She took the bag out of the closet and laid it gently on the bed, unzipping the zip as if it was Pandora's box. But nothing emerged from the plastic beyond a wistful sense of nostalgia.

She'd designed the dress herself, going through pages of scrapbook paper until she got it just right, and she'd saved up the money she'd made working weekends for her mom to buy the material. She ran a finger over the fine chiffon, smiling at the memory of paying full price for the fabric so her mom wouldn't know what she was up to. Stolen moments she'd worked at it, measuring, cutting, stitching, while she and Curtis had been making plans. He'd been stashing away enough money to pay for their trip, ready to go the moment she'd had her birthday and was legal.

Lily bit down on her lip as she took the gown out of the bag. In those days she'd designed and sewed many of her own clothes, thinking of opening her own boutique while Curtis worked alongside his father. She'd dreamed of teaching her own daughter to cut and stitch. She unzipped the hidden zipper and stepped into the pristine white creation. She moved the hasp of the zipper upward, sucking in a bit to get it to the top. It fit. It was a little snug in the chest, but her figure was much the same as it had been when she was eighteen and full of dreams.

She went to the mirror and stood, staring at the fine stitch work. Spaghetti straps held the simple bodice, which draped and gathered at the side. The satin underskirt felt luxurious against her bare legs, while the chiffon fell with a long, soft ruffle down to the hem. Not a pucker or misplaced fold in sight.

Lily raised her arms, gathering the cloud of her hair into a twist, holding it with one hand while her eyes searched the reflection in the mirror.

"Is that Jen's dress?"

Lily jumped at the sound of a deep voice, releasing her hair in a tumble about her shoulders and catching her toe in the folds of the skirt.

"Noah!"

"You must not have heard me knock."

She pressed a hand to her heart, supremely embarrassed that he had found her in such a state. "So you just came in?"

"The door was unlocked. I saw your car and figured you were home. I take it your guests are gone?" He took a hesitant step inside her room, not waiting for her answer. "That's beautiful."

The compliment both touched her and cut like a knife. "You could have knocked harder," she snapped. The last thing she needed was Noah prying. If she'd heard the knock, she could have at least scrambled out of the gown and into her jeans again. She'd never meant for anyone to actually *see* her in the dress. Let alone the man she hadn't been able to erase from her thoughts. The memory of their kiss was stuck in her brain with disturbing clarity.

"I'm sorry. I wanted to show you something." His eyes looked sincere enough. Lily let out a breath and told herself to relax.

"Show me something?"

He nodded, a slow smile lighting his face making him look years younger. "I came to take you for a ride."

Lily understood immediately where the little boy smile had come from. "You finally got your truck."

"Yup."

"And you came to show it off."

"Yup."

"And I suppose taking Andrew or Jen for a drive wouldn't have sufficed." She grabbed at the opportunity for distraction, taking the focus off her appearance. He looked so hopeful she couldn't resist teasing him just a bit.

"I got it yesterday and drove the boys to the golf course today. I'm just on my way home and thought I'd stop."

She had to turn away from the pride in his voice. She was happy for him. Not being able to get around on his own had limited his freedom, and she understood how difficult it must have been for a man like him, who was used to being self-reliant. And yet she was reminded that every step of his recovery was one step further to his getting on with his life, and here she was, pathetically dressed up in a wedding dress that should never have seen the light of day again. She wished she'd never taken the garment bag out of the closet.

"Come for a drive with me, Lily."

There was something in his voice that called to her even though she couldn't say exactly what it was. But it almost sounded like need, a little thread of tension through the celebratory facade.

And as much as she'd never admit it out loud, she liked being needed. Even if this development put him one step closer to being out of her life.

She twisted her fingers together, hating the mix of feelings that seemed to keep cropping up with planning Jen and Andrew's big day. She'd been contented here, buying her house, settling into her job, making friends. She'd even managed to avoid talk of babies and marriage and dating. Now Lucy was nearly due and Jen was alight with nuptial plans and she couldn't escape Noah even when she tried. Not that she'd tried very hard.

A few hours driving in a truck with Noah, away from white dresses and shower leftovers sounded very nearly like a perfect way to spend an afternoon.

"Just let me change," she replied softly. The sooner this gown was off and put away, the better. It had been a stupid thing to do, to take it out and try it on in the first place. Even if she did now remember how to fix the skirt.

"I'll wait, then," he answered.

Lily inhaled and exhaled twice, trying to calm her nerves as Noah's steps sounded on the stairs. He'd sought her out, as a friend. As someone to spend some time with. That was all.

She had to remember that he had apologized for making the mistake of kissing her. *She* was the one making a lot of something out of nothing, only because she was attracted to him. She stared at her reflection one last time.

Maybe she should simply relax. What was the harm in spending time, enjoying his company? She didn't have to worry about him falling in love or wanting anything more permanent that she wasn't capable of. It seemed pretty clear that he didn't think of her in *that way.*

And maybe she should just stop thinking, full stop. She pulled at the zipper and it slid down a few inches before getting jammed. Lily closed her eyes, told herself to relax and tried jiggling it up and down. How could it be stuck? It might have something to do with the fact that it was slightly too tight, she grimaced. She sucked everything in as best she could, but nothing. It was well and truly caught.

She went to the door and called downstairs. "Noah? You still there?"

"Yeah." She heard his voice come from the kitchen and she sighed.

"I seem to have run into a snag."

He came to the bottom of the stairs and looked

up. He wore a plain T-shirt today in black, a pair of faded jeans hugging his lower body. Her eyes fell on his stump sock and she realized that working a zipper wasn't going to be easy for him, either.

"I've caught the zip."

He grinned. "Oh, dear."

Now he was teasing! Infernal man. And when had he developed dimples? She didn't seem to remember that detail before, but as he grinned up at her she saw two subtle indentations mocking her.

"Could you help? Please?"

"Since you asked so nicely…"

He came up the stairs toward her and she got a warm curl right in the center of her belly. He was coming to help with the dress, nothing more, but seeing him take the stairs one at a time, coming to her bedroom, seemed very intimate indeed. Her tongue darted out and wet her lips.

Noah reached the top step, stopping directly in front of her. She tilted her chin up to see his face. There was something in his eyes she hadn't seen before. The blue was deeper, the pupils larger, drawing her into the dark shadows, making her wonder what was behind them. Desire pulsed through her, shocking her with its potency as her well-intentioned self-talk went flying off on the summer breeze.

"Turn around," he commanded, the words soft but an order just the same, and she obeyed, giving her back to him, reaching behind and pulling her hair over her shoulder. His fingers toyed with the clasp and she realized that she was very happy for the fact that this dress, unlike Jen's, wasn't strapless. She wasn't wearing a bra underneath. All she was wearing was a pair of plain white bikini panties.

Each breath going into her lungs was torture as his warm fingertips played with the mechanism.

"It's stuck in the lining." Frustration rippled in his voice. "I can't get a good enough hold on it with one hand, and I don't want it to tear."

She nearly told him it didn't matter, but then she would have to explain it was not Jen's dress and she didn't want to open that particular can of worms. "What if you held the lining back and I tried to move the zipper up or down? You can be my eyes, tell me which way to go."

He pinched the fabric and she extended her

right arm behind to grip the zipper. "Move it up," he said, and all the while she could feel the heat of his body oh-so-close to hers. Trying to suck things in was even harder when it felt as though every cell in her body was expanding.

She pulled up, felt it give a little.

"Down, just a bit, then up again."

She obeyed, following his directions, until his fingers closed over hers and pulled the zipper down. All the way down, to where it ended at the hollow of her spine.

Noah focused on the fabric caught in the mechanism rather than on the delicious curve of her neck. He wanted to kiss it something awful, but she was already wound up tight and tense all over. Knowing it set his body on fire, and he forced himself to concentrate on the zipper and not the pale skin revealed by the cut of the dress. Even pinching the fabric was proving difficult, and required all his attention.

But seeing her in a wedding gown had damn near gutted him, even if it wasn't her own. He'd never seen anything so beautiful, and knowing Lily had made it with her own hands had only added to its charm. Marriage had never even been on his radar, but Lily made him start to understand the attraction. He didn't know why she had Jen's dress on, but Andrew's eyeballs were going to be knocked out at the wedding.

The way his were right now as together they pulled the zipper to the bottom and a wedge of creamy white back was revealed to his gaze. The fact that she wasn't wearing a bra only fueled the flames.

The dress gaped at the waist and he caught a tempting glimpse of skimpy white underwear. She had two tiny dimples at the top of her tailbone. He wanted to touch them with a finger. Wanted to touch the skin that was scented with vanilla and almond.

But undressing a woman in a wedding gown was something he never intended to do. And now, with his body scarred and disfigured, he knew he had to step away. She'd made it clear each time she backed off that she wasn't interested in him in *that* way. And could he blame her? He had a difficult enough time dealing with his injuries. It was different for a lover. There were some things you could never expect a woman to overcome.

He stepped back, swallowing hard, exerting restraint and keeping his fingers to himself. "There you go. Good as new. I'll wait for you downstairs."

Lily heard his footsteps muffled on the carpet of the stairs. She gathered the sagging skirt up in her hands and rushed back into the bedroom. She let the gown drop to the floor and hurriedly shoved on her jeans and put on a bra and light sweater. Good as new indeed. If he only knew.

She'd wanted him to touch her, so badly she had ached. She'd wanted to feel his fingers on her skin, wanted him to slide the straps off her shoulders and she'd wanted to turn into his embrace, feeling his warm body against hers.

But he'd turned away, and she just thanked God she hadn't been brazen enough to do it and make a fool of herself. Clearly he was not feeling the same incendiary attraction that she was.

She had to stop thinking of him this way. He'd made it clear that Lazy L was just a pit stop on the road to his recovery, and that was just fine with her. But she couldn't get him out of her mind. And she wasn't thinking about him in a best man kind of way....

Now he was waiting for her to go for a drive,

and her body was still humming from the simple contact of his fingers on her skin. How could she possibly go with him? But if she backed out now he'd know how desperately he'd affected her. No, she had to go downstairs and act as if nothing had happened. She grabbed a hair elastic and wound her hair into a ponytail. She would go for a drive with him. They would have *fun* and forget all about this one-sided sexual attraction business. And she would not allow herself to feel let down that instead of kissing her again as she wanted, he had walked away.

It was for the best. Kissing Noah wouldn't lead anywhere.

When she went downstairs she found him outside on the deck, looking at the long range of mountains to the west. "Sorry about the mess," she said, going out to meet him.

"That's all right. I was just admiring the view." He didn't look at her, just rested his elbow on the wood railing while the sun glinted off his hair. "How'd the shower go?"

"Oh, as you'd expect. Lots of women talking about girlie things and a predominance of the color pink." She smiled softly. "You wouldn't have enjoyed it at all."

"You might be surprised. Women and food in one location. It's hard to find a downside."

Lily smiled shyly, remembering once again how his fingers had felt on her skin. "Noah Laramie, are you flirting with the maid of honor?"

He paused for a minute, as if deliberating an answer. What he said wasn't at all what she expected.

"It's been a long day. I felt the need to get away."

Somehow Lily found the courage to ask what she was dying to know. "So you came to me?"

"Yeah." He smiled at her, just the hint of his dimple taunting. "Yeah, Lily. I came to you."

Lily struggled to keep everything normal. "You must be relieved to have some measure of freedom these days," she remarked, leaning her elbows on the deck railing, trying to shift the subject. His admission had made her heart beat way too fast. "No more putting up with my driving."

"Your driving wasn't so bad." He smiled, treating her to a sidelong glance before gazing back out over the trees and fields. "But I'm glad I don't have to inconvenience you and Andrew anymore."

"I don't think either of us minded."

He paused for a few moments, as though he was on the verge of saying something but changed his mind. He rolled his thumb in a circle. "Even so. I don't like to be beholden to people."

She wasn't offended by his independent streak anymore; she admired it. Even if it did make him stubborn to deal with at times. At least he knew what he wanted and didn't back away from it.

"So, where are we going?"

He turned away from the view at last. "The mountains. I've been staring at them for nearly a month. With working and appointments and wedding plans, there hasn't been an opportunity to go."

Lily nearly mentioned that if he'd said something she would have taken him, but she didn't want to spoil the moment for him. "Then let's go."

Lily locked the deck door behind them and followed him out the front door, grabbing her purse from a hook and locking that door, as well. It didn't matter how long she was in Larch Valley or how safe she felt…locking her door was a matter of habit. A remnant of the city living she'd experienced all her life.

Noah went to the passenger side of the truck and opened her door. It wasn't fancy, not like Andrew's huge diesel with all the bells and whistles, and it wasn't even brand-new; it was a few years old with some miles on the odometer. It didn't matter to Lily; she knew it represented freedom for Noah. It still had that new car smell from detailing and it suited Noah's needs just fine.

He hopped up into the driver's seat and started the engine. Lily stared at the console as he put the truck into gear. Everything normally on the right-hand side of the steering column was now on the left, within reach of his good arm. A round knob was installed on the wheel for ease of steering. Before hitting the gas, Noah turned his head and looked at her, his expression so full of boyish happiness that she laughed. He seemed almost like a teenager getting a driver's license for the first time.

"This," she said, buckling her seat belt and nodding at the driver's controls, "is pretty cool."

"Isn't it?" He let off the brake and pulled out into the street. "A few mods and I'm ready to go." He turned a corner, heading for the dusty side roads. "You don't mind the scenic route, do you?"

"Not at all."

The roads were paved but without lines or

shoulders, and constructed like a grid, so each one either went north and south or east and west. As they passed through rolling ranchland dotted with spruce trees and grassy fields of beef herds, Noah tilted his head toward the stereo. "You want some music?"

There was a CD in the deck and Lily hit the play button. They enjoyed the day and the music without words for several minutes as they came out at the highway, heading north to Longview. It was nice not to feel the need to make conversation to fill uncomfortable gaps. Noah seemed to enjoy driving so much that she slid down in the seat a bit and crossed her left ankle over her right knee, getting comfortable.

At Longview they turned onto the road leading to Kananaskis and the Peter Lougheed Park. Here the dwellings were even more scattered; at times they drove for miles without seeing a soul. They climbed as the road moved northwest, up through the mountains, sharp faces and peaks and cattle ranging freely. Once they slowed down to watch a gathering of bighorn sheep on the jagged rocks, with ragged coats and little ones with nubbins for horns at their sides. Lily thought of the foal and finally broke the silence.

"How's the baby doing?"

Noah looked over briefly, a smile lighting his face that seemed to heat the cab of the truck. "She's fine. Her mama, too."

"Did Andrew name her?" She knew Jen had christened the mare, and she hoped the baby wasn't called "the foal" all the time. She deserved a proper name.

"I did."

He didn't look away from the road this time, and Lily thought she saw a slight blush infuse his cheeks. "You did? You named an itty-bitty baby horse?"

"You're teasing me."

"I am, yes." She rested her head back on the seat with a smug smile. "So, what did you name her?"

"Gorgeous."

Lily laughed. "Beautiful… Gorgeous…it fits. Bit sentimental for a tough old soldier like you, though, don't you think?"

He pulled into a lay-by spot at the crest of Highwood Pass and put the truck into Park. He half turned on his seat to face her. "Is that how you see me? A tough old soldier?"

He wasn't smiling anymore. She wondered if she'd hit a nerve or if there was something bothering him, as she'd suspected earlier. "I don't know. Sometimes."

He turned off the ignition and opened the door to the truck, sliding out and shutting it, leaving her sitting alone.

There was something bothering him. Something beyond dealing with his injury. Lily got out of the truck, too, and followed him to the edge of the paved parking space. She hesitated. The earlier lightheartedness of going for a drive was gone, and instead he was very nearly unapproachable. She was getting used to his mood swings by now. If he had sought her out rather than his brother or even Jen, then there had to be a reason.

She went to him and laid a hand in the space between his shoulder blades. "What's wrong?"

The muscles were so tense beneath her fingers. Had he had bad news? Was it to do with his latest physio appointment? The change had occurred when she'd called him a tough old soldier. She rubbed gently. "Noah, what's happened? Is there something wrong with your recovery?"

He shook his head. "No, nothing like that. Physio is going well."

"Then what?"

He turned to face her. "How much do you know about Andrew? About our parents?"

"I know that your mother left when you were very young and your father raised you."

He nodded, but his lips formed such a thin, forbidding line Lily knew there was more to the story. "Is this to do with your parents?"

"I'm not sure it's for me to tell."

She reached out and grabbed his wrist. "If you didn't want to tell me, you wouldn't have brought me here. You might as well come out with it."

The tense lines of his face eased a little. "There's that practical streak again."

"You can thank me for it later." She softened as his eyes seemed to ask her to understand even though he hadn't yet said the words. "Let me help you, Noah."

"Andrew dropped a couple of bombshells the night Gorgeous was born. One is that Gerald was not his father. We're only half brothers."

Lily tried to hide her shock. Jen hadn't breathed a word, and she knew from talk around town that Andrew had always been considered Gerald Laramie's upstart boy. But for Noah not to have known…and especially now, when family was so important.

"And does that change anything for you?"

"Of course!" He pulled his arm away from her hand. "No, not really. I don't know."

"What does it change?"

"Everything I thought I knew. Andrew's known since high school, and yet no one bothered to say a thing to me. If I'd known…"

"Ah yes." Lily had played this game often enough and could guess what was going through his mind. "If I'd only, right? Only there is no point because the past cannot be changed." She knew that well enough, too. Just as much as she knew letting go was easier said than done. "Does it change how you feel about Andrew?"

"Of course not!" He took a step backward. "He's my brother."

"If that's the case, then you will come to terms with the rest. Just give it time."

Noah walked away, kicking at some random stones that were on the asphalt. "Andrew and Jen have invited our mother to the wedding."

Lily's lips dropped open. "The mother who left you when you were children."

"Yes."

"When did you see her last?"

Silence, with the only sound the odd vehicle passing by and the breeze through the grass and fireweed.

"When I was seven."

"Oh, Noah." He didn't have to say any more. This wedding was going to be difficult enough for him. She'd understood that from the start. She knew he didn't much enjoy being out in public, being stared at and whispered about behind hands. In a city of strangers it was bad enough. But in Larch Valley, where everyone seemed to know everything, it was worse. To ask him to stand up at the wedding, knowing the truth, and to face his mother after all these years…

"Are you scared?"

"Scared?" He wrinkled his brow as he stared at her. "Why would I be scared?"

"Of seeing her? It would be understandable." She went to him and laid her hand on his arm.

"She's little more than a stranger to me, Lily. I know why she left. I stopped hating her for it long ago. It was why I joined the army. For a new start."

He stared out over the mountain range, and

Lily felt the wall go up again, the transparent yet tangible barrier of self-protection.

"I didn't come here to talk about my mother."

"Then why did you?"

His gaze plumbed hers for long seconds. "Because today was the hardest day I've had to face yet, and at the end of it…"

He broke off and looked away.

"At the end of it?" She prodded gently, holding her breath, feeling the connection zip between them again, drawing them together.

"At the end of it, the one person that seemed to make sense was you."

CHAPTER SEVEN

LILY TORE HER EYES FROM the green curves of the valley below. Perhaps they weren't so different after all. They'd both made choices based on what they *didn't* want out of life and along the way found a measure of peace in belonging—him within the army and her in Larch Valley. Now all of that was being ripped away bit by bit for Noah. The life he'd made for himself wouldn't ever be quite the same again. Andrew was the only family he had left now that Gerald was gone, and the two of them had held on to this family secret, keeping Noah in the dark. Either way, she didn't know whether to be thrilled or afraid that he had sought her out after a difficult day.

"The afternoon with the guys didn't go well?"

"It went as well as I should have expected." There was a harshness underlying the words.

"What went wrong?

"Andrew loves to golf. I thought it would be a

fun afternoon. The two of us, Clay, Dawson. I would play chauffeur. Some laughs, a few beers and a steak sandwich at the clubhouse, you know?"

"But?" She prompted him to continue. His eyes had turned a steely dark blue that she recognized as his stubborn, frustrated look.

"But I felt like an idiot. I drove the cart and played caddy and laughed along, but the whole time I was thinking about how Andrew had known about this for years and no one had bothered to let me in on the secret. And then I was sitting waiting as everyone else was playing. And I couldn't, because I can't golf with one arm."

"And so you felt useless."

"Yes."

Lily's heart ached for him. Noah was not useless. He had so much to give. So many talents, so much insight and intelligence. She hated that he'd been made to feel less just because he wasn't physically capable of hitting a ball with a silly club.

"Andrew should have seen how hard it would be for you and suggested something else," she replied sharply. "I know, I know," she continued as Noah started to open his mouth. "It's his wedding. But still, Noah. A little consideration.

After all, he's the one that dropped the bomb-shell, too." She put a hand on her hip.

Noah's jaw softened with surprise. "Are you defending me?"

"Someone has to, don't they?"

Without warning, he reached out and pulled her close, against his chest where his heart beat strong and true. A few stones rolled beneath her sneakers as her weight shifted. "Thank you," he whispered into her hair. "I was feeling pretty selfish."

She inhaled deeply, absorbing the scent and warmth of him before standing back from his embrace and looking up. "You? Selfish? There isn't a selfish bone in your body."

He shook his head slightly, while his hand still rested at the base of her spine. "Oh, yes, I am. I've done nothing but think of myself lately."

"You earned that right."

"It struck me today that I've avoided town, avoided people, because I'm different now. People look at me differently, talk to me differ-ently. It's why I hesitated when Andrew asked me to be his best man. Today I got a taste of how it will feel to be up at the front of that church. Like I'm on display."

Noah always seemed so take charge; hearing him voice his insecurities surprised and touched her.

"You never felt like that in the army?"

"In the army you're all in there together. Take a look at my company picture sometime. We all look…"

"Alike," she finished. "Did you tell Andrew how you felt about it at all?"

He shook his head again. "Not really. I just let it ride."

A van pulled into the parking lot and Noah removed his hand from her back, their cocoon of privacy broken. They walked back to the truck, pausing and leaning up against the hood as the summer breeze ruffled her hair, sending little pieces scattering out of her ponytail.

"So you asked me to come with you…"

"I needed to talk."

A small smile crept up Lily's cheek. Beyond any of the times she'd nearly died from wanting his touch, at this moment right now she felt closer to Noah than she had since they'd met. Closer than today when he'd seen her in the dress, or in the barn or at his house or measuring tuxedos. Did he realize how silly it sounded?

He was a champion at keeping his feelings to himself. She supposed it had to do with the macho idea that men didn't discuss their feelings. And yet he'd wanted to talk. To her. For some reason it meant a lot for him to tell her why.

"Why me, Noah? Why not Andrew, or Jen?" She asked it quietly, then held her breath.

The answer didn't come right away. The van unloaded a group of tourists who were not concerned with Noah and Lily but more about taking a picture by the sign that marked Highwood Pass's claim to fame—the highest paved point in Canada. Noah ignored them, instead murmuring softly, "Come here."

Lily obeyed, taking his hand, and he moved her to a spot in front of him. His arm came around her, pulling her back against his body that still leaned against the truck, tucking her head beneath his chin. It felt good to be held. Safe and secure and wanted.

"I told you because I trust you, Lily. Not sure why. I'm not even sure how. Maybe because you didn't grow up here and it's easier. Maybe because you always tell me the truth. But I trust you."

Lily closed her eyes. It was true that when

they spoke she was very plain. But there were so many things she hadn't told him. Things she didn't want him to know. Things she hadn't wanted anyone to know. Even Jen knew nothing about Curtis, or why she and her mother had become estranged. And Jen was the closest thing she had to family.

And yet, she trusted him, too. Noah would never judge her. She knew it as surely as she knew this wedding was going to be difficult for both of them.

"I don't like weddings, either." She admitted it and instantly felt better. Somehow with Noah she could stop pretending.

"You don't?" His head moved against hers as if he were trying to peer around to see her expression.

She let out a light laugh. "No, I don't."

"But you are always helping Jen and making the dress and seemed, I don't know, excited."

How could she explain that while she loved her life here, sometimes she still felt the need to put a happy face on for the world? That the woman people saw wasn't the true Lily? She kept that part of her locked up safe and sound.

"Jen is my best friend and it's my problem, not hers. I wouldn't upset her for the world. Just like you didn't want to lay it on Andrew. You grin and fake it. Today's shower was one of the hardest things I've ever had to do."

"Fine pair we make."

"Do you suppose they knew how much trouble we'd be when they asked us?"

Noah laughed, the motion bumping against her back and she leaned more into his shoulder. He gasped slightly at the contact, and Lily felt a quick panic, wondering if she'd hurt him accidentally.

But if she had, he didn't let on. "I thought all women dreamed of weddings."

Ah, there it was. Lily blinked, the words sitting on her tongue. She could explain about the dress today, about the hurt that had never quite gone away. But in the end she couldn't do it. Not all of it.

"My mom never got married. In fact…I never even met my father. She was always, oh, I don't know, open to opportunities. More of a free spirit. Still is. But I think that's when I started hating weddings. At first it was my friends being flower girls. And then just…resenting her, I suppose. She was a seamstress, you know. She'd make these gorgeous dresses, but they were never for her. They would hang on the rack, all white and lacy and shining and all I wanted was for her to put one on and get married and settle us down, instead of moving from place to place all the time. I used to wonder why she spent hours on something she believed so little in. But her motto has always been to love deep and love often. And I suppose she did it because they were beautiful and because it paid the bills."

Noah squeezed her close. "I didn't know. You sound like you were a very lonely girl."

Lily clung to the words and to the feel of his strength surrounding her. "I suppose I was. It was always a different apartment, a different school, new kids. It was why I fell in love with Larch Valley. For the first time in my life I felt like I belonged somewhere. And I'll do this for Jen—dress up in a pink dress and carry flowers and craft centerpieces—because she's the family I found here."

"And I am…?"

The words hung in the air as the tourists piled back in their van and pulled out of the lot.

"You are someone who needed a friend. And you are Andrew's brother, so that makes you family, too."

"I don't want to be an obligation to you."

"You've never been an obligation." Her heart stuttered as she blurted it out, a fearful beat that suggested maybe she'd admitted a little too much. "Do you know what I see when I look at you, Noah? I don't see your limitations. I see a strong, determined man, and before you know it you will be going back to the life you love, too."

A lump formed in her throat at the last words. It was the danger of getting to know someone. Of caring. They always had another life waiting somewhere, didn't they. She'd known from the start he was merely recuperating. That he had every intention of going back to his life in the army. And why shouldn't he reclaim his life?

But she'd let herself get close anyway. It didn't matter how many times she'd told herself it was for the best. Heck, she'd even convinced herself that knowing he would be going back to active duty made him safe. He would not ask for more than she could give.

She turned within his embrace, so she was facing him. For a few moments their gazes caught and held, and they both knew there was more than friendship—obligatory or not—at work. And then a recognition that the inevitable must happen in the end. He was a soldier. It wasn't something he could just quit. It was as much *who* he was as *what* he was.

"So," she said quietly, "we'll get each other through it. You'll grin and bear it. And you can look at me and remember I really dislike the color 'petal pink' and the smell of lilies."

"It's a deal."

She stepped out of his embrace, knowing she must and yet wanting so much more. Perhaps it was enough that they'd silently seemed to acknowledge the attraction. Now it was dealt with and maybe even put aside for the greater good.

But as they got back in the truck and headed home, Lily could only remember how good she'd felt being held by him and how close she'd come to telling him the real reason she dreaded weddings so much.

The platter of grilled steaks was down to juices on the plate and the tray of brownies mere crumbs when Noah approached her. The rehearsal party was winding down, now reduced to wandering with cups of coffee or tea. Lily had helped Jen set it up right here at Lazy L—two of the new tables Jen had bought for the balcony seating at Snickerdoodles, white linens and fresh-cut flowers that Lily had snipped from Agnes Dodds's considerable garden. She'd visited with Mr. and Mrs. O'Keefe, chatted to the minister and his wife, made plans for the following day with Jen.

And the whole time, all she could think about was Noah, and how he'd confided in her, and how much she wanted to feel his arm around her again.

"Do you want to get out of here?" Noah's rough voice tickled her ear.

The low invitation sent her pulse fluttering. "I can't yet. I promised Jen I'd help clear up."

"I need your help with something. I can wait for you."

She smiled then, letting the end-of-the-day warmth and the relaxed atmosphere woo her. "Oooh, mysterious."

He chuckled, the sound low and sexy. Lily looked at him, liking dressed-up Noah. Not the jeans and T-shirts of his everyday life, nor the formality of the tux tomorrow, but a pair of chocolate-brown cotton pants and a lightweight tan shirt. The cuff was rolled up on his left arm, the other side pinned to hide the end of his stump. She stacked a few more plates and angled him a questioning look. "Dare I ask how you rolled up your sleeve, Mr. Laramie?"

"I don't suppose you'd believe me if I said my teeth."

She snorted and then bit down on her lip. "Funny. But no." She turned, holding the plates before her and smiling up into his face. "You are much easier to be around when you are not so grumpy."

"I must be losing my touch."

Hardly, Lily thought as she forced herself to slide away, taking the dishes to the kitchen. Since they'd gone for that drive, he seemed to be more in his stride than ever. Maybe talking had helped restore some of his confidence. He certainly had a way of keeping her attention.

Mrs. O'Keefe was drying the last of the glasses when Lily poured herself a cup of tea. The brew was hot and soothing and she took a moment, listening to the mother-daughter chatter about plans and big days, and for the first time in years she missed her own mother. She missed the Saturday afternoons when Jasmine had made tea and they'd baked butter cookies. Or when she was older, sitting with sketch pads together, designing clothes, stealing ideas from each other's drawings. Her mother had always encouraged Lily's sense of daring and adventure. But the moment Lily had dared to actually use it, the result had been disastrous. Jasmine had been the first one to point out what a horrible mistake she'd made. And Lily had never picked up a sketch pad again.

"Lily?"

Jen's voice pulled her out of her woolgathering and she forced a smile. "Sorry?"

Jen came over and took Lily's empty cup. "You need to go home. We can't have a tired maid of honor tomorrow."

"But I am supposed to help you." She shook off the memories and smoothed her hands down her skirt. "Not the other way around."

"It's nearly done now anyway. And Mom's here. And I'm running on adrenaline anyway." Jen's face was lit up like a candle, glowing with happiness. "You've done so much. The dress…" For a second Lily was afraid Jen was going to cry. But the wobbly smile straightened. "The gown is perfect. Just be at my house at two, ready to get dressed, okay?"

"Okay." Lily was helpless in the face of so much happiness. She didn't begrudge her friend one iota of it. She gave Jen a quick hug. "I'll be there."

She looked out the kitchen window. Noah was climbing into his truck, but he paused and gazed back at the house, as though he was looking for her, asking her to follow him. She took her purse from a hook behind the door and wished everyone a good-night. Went to her car and got in behind the wheel. Drove into town and down the main drag toward her subdivision at the far west end.

But partway there she turned south, headed toward the little gray house where she knew he was waiting. He had asked for her help. And as much as it frightened her, she knew that whenever Noah asked for her, she'd be there.

Noah's truck was parked in the driveway and Lily pulled in behind it. He'd said he needed help with something. Considering the wedding was tomorrow, she hoped it had nothing to do with his tuxedo. His continuing therapy meant he was getting stronger, and the work on the ranch had kept him in shape. But surely everything still fit. The measurements had only been taken a little over a month ago.

The door was unlocked, and Lily walked through the quiet house to the back door. She found him sitting on the step, his arm folded over his knee as he stared past the back fence to the line of shrubs marking the back alley.

"Nice night," she commented softly.

"We survived."

"It helped having a partner in crime."

Lily smiled, sitting down beside him, the hem of her skirt tickling the back of her ankles. Noah had stood beside Andrew at the front of the church as the pianist played a Rachmaninov rhapsody and the minister issued directions as she was walking. It had all felt scripted and silly and with his back to the minister, Noah had rolled his eyes at her, making her smile bloom. They'd walked through the order of service and then it had been over. Jen's mom had placed the simple pew markers on the ends of the benches during the rehearsal, and in the morning, Kristin, the local florist, would deliver the floral arrangements. It had been particularly well-organized in true Jen fashion.

As she sat next to Noah, saying nothing in the twilight, she felt an emptiness open inside her. These moments happened more and more often as Jen's big day approached. Lily had never had a wedding rehearsal. Never had pew markers or special cloths for tables or a maid of honor. And she'd been okay with it, because she and Curtis had made their own plans.

She sighed. She would get through tomorrow.

At her sigh, Noah shifted over a few inches closer and put his arm around her, pulling her close so that her head fit into the curve of his shoulder.

She wasn't the only one dreading the formalities. Somehow they'd both get through it. She'd make sure of it.

"Busy day today." He spoke quietly; it fit the softness of the evening.

"Busier one tomorrow. First the ceremony and then the reception and dance."

"Yeah."

"So what's the emergency?" She stayed where she was, wanting just a few minutes more of the accord she seemed to find when she was in his embrace. "You said you needed help with something. Is it the tux?"

"No, the suit's great. They even pinned the sleeves in place during the final fitting. All I need to do is put it on. It's…" He hesitated. "It's the dance."

Her mouth formed a round O. "I see."

His breath fanned warmly on her hair as he turned his head the slightest bit. "I never thought of it until today when Jen was talking about Andrew dancing with her mother and she with her father tomorrow night...and I realized that I'll probably have obligations, as well."

"Not if you don't want to. I'm sure if you explain...Jen won't hold you to those traditions."

"I still have two legs, Lily. And I work really hard to avoid anyone making allowances for me. Or excuses."

"Don't I know it." It was one of the things that drove her crazy—his stubbornness—but also something she admired so much. He worked so hard at being self-reliant.

"We're going to dance together, Lil."

He shortened her name and it sent curls of intimacy spiraling through her. Dancing with him tomorrow would be easy. There would be people there, friends and guests and it was expected. But here, tonight, she was afraid.

"It'll be fine, don't worry," she reassured him lightly.

But at her flippant tone he removed his arm

from around her shoulders and got up from the step, moving inside, leaving her sitting in the cold that settled over the open prairie on a clear night.

She shivered, felt guilty. He had honestly asked for her help and she had brushed him off, simply because she cared about him too much. Because she wanted him at least as much as she *didn't* want him—perhaps more. Because she was *afraid*. Even to her, that reasoning was flawed.

She got up and followed him inside. He was standing in the middle of the living room, the protective wall he tended to build around himself back in place again. What was it that made him so easy for her to read? Why did she want to?

"I'm sorry, Noah. I didn't mean to make light of it. Of course you're self-conscious."

Noah turned, seeing Lily silhouetted by the pale light coming through the back door. Did she really think this was about him being embarrassed about his arm? He couldn't care less. But perhaps it was better this way. Maybe it was better than her knowing that what he really feared was disappointing her tomorrow. She had been there for him for weeks, and he knew she was dreading the wedding as much as he was…. He wanted to leave her with a good memory of the day. She deserved it. Suddenly he stopped caring about what he looked like, or what people said; he just wanted to be able to dance with her and not have it be a disaster. He wasn't even sure if he could hold her properly.

"I can't hold you the traditional way," he admitted. "And I don't want us to try to figure this out in front of a hundred people tomorrow."

"What do you want to do?"

"I want to dance with you."

"Now?" Her lips parted as she took two steps forward. His memory was assaulted by the soft smell of her perfume, a little bit floral, a little bit citrusy as she'd leaned against him outside. He wanted to be that strong man for her, just this once.

"Now," he murmured, closing the distance between them. "Away from everyone. Just you and me." He swallowed, wondering how it was he wanted to confide in her the very reason he was afraid. Wanted to tell her about all the doubts he was having about what he'd done, where his life was going, the upcoming decisions he knew he had to make. It was more than a physical demanding, though there was definitely that aspect. His body's reaction to her was loud and clear.

The trouble was, he wanted to share everything with her, and he was afraid she'd hand it right back to him with a no-thank-you. How could he expect her to overcome his disfigurement when he could hardly stand to look at himself in the mirror? He couldn't hide the missing arm. But he had successfully hidden the other angry effects of that morning in the desert.

"My right arm is less than half and I…I don't want you to be turned off tomorrow. Hell," he breathed, unable to look into her eyes any longer, turning away from the pity he saw there. "I'd give anything to have two good arms to hold you with right now."

The silence bore down on him until he heard the sound of her steps behind him. There was the click of the stereo and the sound of her putting the remote control down on the shelf. Soft music played quietly behind him and every muscle in his body tensed. He could imagine holding her close, moving their feet together. Why was it that at these moments, he would swear he could still feel his hand, longing to reach out and touch her? To feel her hair between his fingers? He closed his eyes, unable to fight the tingling sensation as his brain's memory warred with reality. Hating it and yet trying to imprint it on his memory anyway.

And then her hand was there, warm against the flat of his back. "Then dance with me, Noah."

Slowly he turned, saw her looking up at him with caring and acceptance. He'd hidden things from her for so long—bouts of phantom pain and discomfort and the annoyances of having to deal with mundane tasks. He'd gotten quite good at it. But now, she held up her right palm and he placed his left one against it as her body came closer to his; only a whisper apart. He could not pull her close as he wanted, and held himself stiffly, hating his injury more now than he had in any moment since he'd awoken in Kandahar after the firefight.

And then Lily reached out with her left hand, slid her arm around his back and pressed her body lightly against his.

He swallowed, wishing for the first time for a prosthetic so he could at least pretend to hold her as a man should.

He cupped her hand in his and shuffled his feet along to the music, feeling her sway with him as they took small steps in the dark living room. In years past, he would have used his right hand to stroke her back, or toy with the hair at the back of her neck. Tonight he could do none of those things. Tonight he was more attracted to her than he'd ever been to any woman, and he was helpless to do anything about it, even as they quietly moved in a slow circle. Tonight he wanted to explain to her about all his injuries, to show his scars. But to do that would be sending her away, and he couldn't do it. Not yet. So he prayed that she held on and that the song wouldn't end too soon.

Lily bit down on her lip, the feelings pulsing through her raw and real. She'd realized right away that by holding her right hand traditionally, he would not have a hand to put at her waist. Instead, she'd put hers around him, moving carefully so she wouldn't bump his arm. As a solo voice and guitar wooed the air around them, their feet had started moving, and his fingers had tightened over hers almost painfully.

He could have simply gone against tradition

and not danced tomorrow. But instead he was allowing himself to be vulnerable, to do something despite his disability, despite how it would look. She was glad…so glad. Being held against him, swaying with him in the dark was the sweetest thing she'd ever known.

Her hand slid up his right shoulder blade, stroking against the cotton, every fibre in her body vibrating with life, like smooth ripples on a pond. With a mixture of wonderment and fear, she let her fingers glide over the crest of his shoulder and slowly, testing, over the tricep of his arm, to where she felt the silicone cap beneath his shirt.

His muscles tightened beneath her touch, his whole body alert, and she held her breath, moving her fingertips back to the line of his shoulder, up to his neck, across the line where his hair met his collar. And back down again, wanting, needing to know all of him.

"Lily," he whispered, but she cut off any refusal he could utter.

"I don't want to pretend it doesn't exist," she whispered, letting her hand rest where his collarbone met his shoulder. "It's part of who you are."

"Only a part," he whispered bitterly, his feet halting.

But she looked up at him, his dark eyes mere shadows shining down at her. "Yes, Noah. Only one part. Why won't you share it with me?"

He seemed to struggle for a few moments for an answer. When it came, his voice was rough and raw, as if it physically hurt to speak.

"Because I want to be perfect for you."

At that moment, Lily felt herself going. Sliding out of the life she'd built for herself into a place so painfully sweet it stole her breath. There was nothing she could do to stop the rush of feeling.

"You are," she whispered. She took her hand from his and framed his face with her fingers. "Oh, Noah, you are."

His eyes glittered at her as the music stopped. With his left arm free, he looped it around her waist and pulled her against his chest. Then he lowered his head and kissed her until all the reasons against them scattered like the stars.

CHAPTER EIGHT

"You look beautiful, Jen."

Lily stood back, staring at her best friend, who simply beamed as she stood in the middle of the bedroom. Lily blinked back a small tear as the photographer snapped a candid photo of the two of them together. The intrusion was a welcome one for Lily. The last thing she wanted to do was get overly emotional today. Knowing there was always the chance of being snapped, she kept her features well schooled.

Jen reached out and took her hand. "And so do you. The dresses are so lovely, Lily. I can't thank you enough."

Lily felt the sting again and covered it by giving Jen a quick hug. "You are a gorgeous and happy bride," she whispered. "That's all the thanks I need."

She turned away and retrieved the bouquets still sitting in their tissue and boxes on the bed.

"Now you are ready. I have the ring and you have your flowers and there is a surprise for you outside."

"A surprise?" Jen rushed to the window. "Oh, Lily!"

Lily smiled. "We can't have you going to the wedding in my old car, can we? We're going to ride in style. But she's not much for speed. We should get going."

With a delighted giggle, Jen rushed to the door and outside, holding up her tiny train as she tripped down the walk. Lily sighed and followed, carrying a small bag with makeup fixes and the ring. Outside she met Jen by the side of a horse-drawn black buggy.

"Wherever did it come from?"

Lily laughed, she couldn't help it. Jen had planned the day meticulously, but she hadn't suspected a thing. "Mrs. Dodds knows a lot of people. It's from Noah and me."

"You two…" Jen paused, her hand in the driver's and her toes on the foot plate. "You really are a pair, aren't you."

Lily shook her head, denying the flash of elation she felt at being paired up with Noah for real. She motioned for the driver to help Jen up to the seat. "No, we're not," she replied, following suit and settling on the cushioned seat. She refused to let Jen see how complicated it all was. Especially after last night. The memory of those few stolen minutes still made her dizzy. Remembering his mouth on hers, or the way his arm had pulled her tight against his muscled body. "We're friends, that's all. That's what you said you wanted," she reminded Jen. The last thing she wanted was for Jen to know she and Noah had kissed. More than once. It was fragile enough without outside interference.

With a flick of the reins by the driver, the buggy jolted and they were on their way.

"Besides," Lily continued before Jen could reply, "today is your day. Your wedding. Noah and I should be way down on your list of discussable topics."

"I can't believe it's happening." Jen's hands fidgeted in her lap. "For so many years, I thought we'd lost our chance, you know?" Jen's eyes lit with anticipation.

Lily smiled, pushing back the bittersweet memory of her own wedding excitement only moments before it had gone so desperately wrong. Jen would have a perfect day. Lily would make sure of it.

"Are you nervous?"

"A little." Jen pressed her hand to her belly. "I don't know why. I've wanted this since forever."

"Just remember who is waiting for you at the end of the aisle," Lily advised, running a hand over the skirt of her pink dress. Noah would be standing at the front with Andrew. Noah would be in his tuxedo. The same Noah who had held her and danced with her and kissed her last night until she was sure her heart would break with love. The strong, irascible man had shown her his vulnerable side. And it had turned everything she thought she knew on its head.

Noah.

"Oh, Lily, listen!"

The church bells were clanging in the summer breeze and Lily's smile wobbled. It wasn't fair to make comparisons. But when had life truly been fair? She wouldn't begrudge her friend this moment for all the world. But it wasn't fair that Lily had been cheated out of one wedding, and it wasn't fair that now, when she finally fell in love again, it was with the wrong man.

They pulled up to the church as the bells

ceased pealing, the photographer pulling up
behind in his car and getting out. "Give me a few
minutes to get into position," he instructed,
while Jen's mom and dad waited on the church
steps.

Lily got out of the carriage and took Jen's
flowers while she got down, holding the skirt
gingerly and revealing white satin pumps. Lily
straightened the gown, then brushed her hand
down her own, smoothing out any wrinkles. It
had been Jen's wish that they both wear strapless gowns, but Lily suddenly felt self-conscious
in the obvious concession to femininity. What
would Noah think, seeing the floor-length pink
confection? How would he look at her as she
stepped onto the navy carpet runner? Things
between them hadn't ended well last night. She
had apologized, of all things, stammering and
babbling while he stood motionless in the center
of the room. She'd had her hand on the doorknob
when he'd finally spoken, saying her name and
how he would see her at the wedding.

He'd been in control, and she'd felt all at sea
and needing to run. Or at least she thought he'd
been in control.

She arranged her hair over her shoulders,

making sure the pearl-headed pins holding back several curls were secure. What would he say the moment he took her arm to leave the church? And then there were pictures, and being seated together, and…

Her breaths shallowed and she felt slightly light-headed. Oh, this would never do. She couldn't truly be in love with him, she decided. It was the wedding spinning a spell, weaving fanciful magic. It was all the time they'd spent together, that was all. She'd been careful not to go out on more than a few dates with any one man for years, avoiding entanglement.

But that had all changed when her best friend had asked for a favor. And perhaps that long drought had made her thirsty. And Noah was too tempting to resist.

The fact remained that he would be returning to his army life. It had just been last night, and the wedding preparations, and the music in the dark. It would have enchanted anyone. He had kissed her, that was all.

She squared her shoulders, inhaling deeply, the scent of flowers and fresh-cut hay and sunshine filling her nostrils as she climbed the church steps ahead of Lily and her parents. She hid the bag of makeup beneath the guest book table, removing the large gold wedding band and slipping it over her thumb for safekeeping. She smiled at Andrew's friends, Clay and Dawson, who were in suits rather than jeans and boots, and acting as ushers today. Clay threw her a wink as he stepped inside the sanctuary door, escorting Mrs. O'Keefe to her seat while the pianist played something soft and pretty.

And then the music stopped and Clay and Dawson took their own seats.

Lily turned to Jen, who was already holding her father's arm, and adjusted the simple veil over Jen's shoulders. "See you at the front," she whispered, smiling.

She turned and took the first step onto the carpet, clutching her bouquet until her knuckles turned white.

Andrew was there, standing at the bottom of the steps, but it wasn't his face that held her attention. It was Noah's, beside him, his deep blue gaze warm with something so intimate she felt herself flush all over. The makings of a smile flirted with the corners of his mouth as his eyes telegraphed his approval. *You look beautiful,* they seemed to say. She blinked, wondering why on earth she should feel the need to cry walking up the aisle as a bridesmaid.

And oh, he looked so handsome, so straight and tall, his broad chest highlighted by the cut of the jacket and the white tie bobbing at his throat as he swallowed.

Then she was at the front, on the other side of the altar from him, and with a shaky breath, she turned her attention to the woman at the door of the church.

The music swelled and the congregation rose as Jen entered, the town sweetheart, the woman who had somehow wound herself into the hearts of everyone present. Lily couldn't help the smile that lit her face when Jen's and Andrew's gazes met, so filled with love and hope.

Something made her glance over at Noah and she saw a tiny wrinkle in his brow. He stared at Jen and then looked over at Lily, a question in his eyes. She had hoped he wouldn't remember. Wouldn't recall that the dress she'd worn that day had been different. But he hadn't just seen it, he'd touched it, the tiny straps and the zipper along her back. She shivered as she remembered his fingers on her skin.

The minister opened with a prayer and the

giving away of the bride. He asked the question—if anyone opposed the marriage they should speak now—and Lily froze, her heartbeat stuttering as her fingers clenched the roses and sweet peas painfully. This was where her own fairy tale had ended. She bit her lip and tried to focus on the minister's words instead of her memories, but it didn't work. The flurry of excitement, the angry words, the tears. She had never spoken the vows, or put on the plain gold ring, or tasted the first kiss of marriage. It had all ended with a single word. *If anyone has reason why these two should not be joined... Yes.*

But the minister moved on and the rest of the ceremony happened in a daze. Lily held Jen's bouquet during the vows, and while she and Andrew sealed their marriage with a first kiss. She saw Andrew's lashes fall as he leaned in, and an image of Noah in the dark flashed through her mind like heat lightning. Her lips tingled, remembering how she'd melted against him, let him into all the dark corners of her heart, how little fingers of need had clung to him even as the kiss had softly ended. Their eyes met while Jen and Andrew kissed, and Lily knew he hadn't forgotten, either. His hooded gaze dropped to her lips and back up, leaving her as breathless as if he'd kissed her.

A soloist from the church sang as Jen and Andrew signed the wedding register. Then it was Lily's turn, and Noah's. He held her flowers as she sat at the small table, signing her name on the witness lines. She tried not to think of how sexy he looked, all done up in his tux, holding a posy of white peony roses and pale pink sweet peas. When she finished, she met his eyes briefly as she took back the flowers, their fingers grazing. The slight contact played havoc with her senses, a jolt from her fingertips to her core. She watched, fascinated, as his tongue came out to wet his lips.

She wondered how on earth it could feel as if they'd held a conversation over the past half hour when the ceremony had prevented either of them from uttering a word.

Then he moved away, taking his place at the table and with concentrated effort, signed his name where designated. Lily noticed the letters were much neater than before. Day by day he was improving. Day by day he was one step closer to rejoining his life.

And then the ceremony was over, and her fingers gripped her bouquet tightly as her right hand rested on Noah's arm. Amidst the recessional and the clapping, they made their way down the aisle and into the bright sunshine.

There were a blessed few moments where confusion reigned as the church emptied. Noah shifted his arm, catching Lily's fingers within his own instead. "You look amazing," he murmured, leaning close to her ear as guests spilled out into the parking lot and green grass surrounding the church.

Lily smiled up at him, determined to put things back on an even footing. "Thank you. And you look very dashing."

He smiled back briefly, but then it faded. "Lily, about last night…"

She felt that familiar turning in her tummy that happened every time he spoke to her with that soft, but gruff voice. And yet the day was difficult enough without adding their troubles to it. "Let's just forget it," she suggested. "Why don't we try to enjoy the day? We're partners in crime, remember?" She let her eyes twinkle up at him. "It isn't right to admit to hating weddings while you're attending one, I suppose."

"So you're just using me to survive the festivities?"

If he only knew. But the truth was, even if she did feel something for him she had never expected to feel again, nothing had changed. What did she want from him? Certainly not marriage. The very idea sent an ache pulsing through her, and a panicky need to keep things as uncomplicated as possible.

"Why don't we just enjoy each other?" Lily saw the photographer bearing down on them and squeezed his hand. "We're friends, and I like you. A lot, in case you didn't notice." She attempted a saucy smile. "Let's just leave it at that. Can't we have fun in the time we have?" If he caught the note of desperation in her voice, he ignored it.

Noah paused, and their gazes tangled for a few moments before his eyes lightened. "Sure we can. Although fun is something that hasn't been on my radar for a while."

"Then maybe it's time."

"Miss Germaine? Mr. Laramie? I need you for wedding party pictures."

Lily gathered her skirt in her fingers. "Come on then. Let's get this over with. I can bear it if you can."

The photographer gave orders, arranging the two couples on the church's stone steps with the large double doors behind them. There were pictures with Lily and Jen together, their skirts and flowers artistically arranged, and shots of the two brothers. There were many photographs with Jen and Andrew while Lily and Noah and the guests that hadn't gone to the community hall for the reception watched. One woman stood alone from the others, slim and almost drawn within herself, as though she was trying to be inconspicuous. But Lily twigged to something about the fine cheekbones, and the deep-set eyes. The resemblance wasn't immediately apparent, but it was there.

"Is that her, Noah?" Lily whispered. "Standing over by the shrubs?"

"Yes, that's her." There was an underlying note of steel in his voice.

"Did you speak to her?"

"And say what? Hello is not enough. And anything more is unthinkable."

Still, he refused to look over at the woman and Lily squeezed his fingers. "You're right."

Andrew called their names again and Noah sighed with irritation. "What happened to fun?

I am duty bound to remind you of the color of your dress. Pink, Lily. Very, very pink."

He winked at her, tugging her hand again and leading her to where the bride and groom waited. "Fun. It's what you said you wanted. So come on."

The photographer wanted pictures of only the maid of honor and best man, and he had chosen the shade of a poplar tree for the shot. Noah leaned lightly against the trunk while Lily rested against his right shoulder, disguising his pinned-up sleeve. She hesitated as his mouth twisted in a grimace, but he quickly gave her an encouraging smile. "It's fine," he murmured, settling her back against the hard length of his body. Noah's left arm looped around her, and in a stroke of ingenuity the photographer had him hold Lily's flowers loosely while she crossed her right hand to rest on his wrist.

"You smell good," he whispered, making her smile.

"It's the sweet peas," she replied, holding the pose for the shot.

"No lilies, Lily?"

"No, thank God. I can't imagine what my mother was thinking when she named me."

"Beautiful, exotic, sweet."

Lily's pulse leaped at the softly whispered words. She couldn't see his face as they held their positions. "Mr. Laramie, I do believe you're flirting."

"You might be right, Miss Germaine."

This was better, Lily thought. Even if her feelings for him were the real deal, what was important was that she didn't act on them. No grand declarations of love or expectations of commitment. A firm belief that this was only temporary. Yes, that was the ticket. The more she thought about it the more sure she was. She could give herself permission to feel. It was human after all, and she wasn't callous or bitter. She simply had made decisions about what she wanted from life. And she had to remember that Noah hadn't said a word about loving *her*. The worries were for nothing.

"Lily? He's asked us to move."

"Oh, right, sorry." She took the bouquet from his hands and smiled brightly. "Are we done here yet? I could use something to drink."

"I'll find out. Two seconds."

He strode back across the lawn toward her. He'd removed his tuxedo jacket and had hooked the collar by a finger, holding it over his shoulder. Lily wet her lips. "Well?"

"We're free to go. Andrew and Jen will be taking the carriage over to the reception. We can take my truck."

"Sounds good to me."

She followed him to the parking lot and gathered her skirt around her as she got up into the cab. Just before he shut the door, he chuckled. "Nice shoes. They're not actually glass slippers, are they?"

Lily flushed. She might not like pink, but she'd been unable to resist the shoes. They were slides, with a transparent band across the top of her foot adorned with a satin ribbon, and a transparent two-inch heel. She knew they were ultrafeminine and fanciful. But she'd adored them the moment she'd slipped them on. "Of course not."

Noah went around to the driver's side door and hopped in. "Okay, Cinderella, let's get you to the ball," he remarked drily, starting the truck and putting it in reverse.

Lily stared out the window to hide her flaming cheeks, somehow feeling she was riding in a pumpkin after all.

* * *

The toasts had been made, the cake cut, and the deejay was playing music quietly until it was time for the first dance to be announced. Lily freshened her makeup and came out of the bathroom to find Noah and his mother, Julie Reid, in a corner, speaking quietly. Lily paused, retreated to where she wouldn't intrude. And yet she wanted to be close by. She recognized the tight set of his jaw and the way his skin seemed taut across his cheekbones as he kept his countenance polite. The words they said were too low to be heard, and she didn't want to eavesdrop. She just wanted to be there.

Julie put her hand on Noah's sleeve but he didn't move to take it. Nor did he pull away. Sympathy flooded through her. Imagine meeting a parent for the first time in over twenty years, and doing it publicly. How would she have reacted if Jasmine had shown up tonight?

But then her lips fell open as Noah smiled at his mother. Not a big smile, but a definite pleasant curving of his lips. She put back her shoulders, pasted on a smile of her own and stepped forward.

"There you are!" She went up to his side and

took his hand, giving his fingers a reassuring squeeze. "The dancing is about to start."

"Lily." His smile got bigger as he said her name. "Lily, this is my mother, Julie Reid." He paused, seemed to struggle for a moment and then simply said, "This is Lily, Jen's maid of honor."

"Hello," the woman said, her smile faltering as she looked a long way up at her son.

"Please excuse us," Noah said politely, nodding at Julie before taking Lily's hand and going back to the reception room.

"How did it go?"

Noah surveyed the room blandly. "Fine, I guess. We're strangers, Lily. We both know it. It wasn't as difficult as you might think. I'm glad she came, to be honest. It's been good for Andrew. Maybe good for me, too."

The deejay announced the first dance and Lily and Noah halted by the cake table, watching Jen and Andrew take the floor, their permanent smiles still bright on their faces, eyes only for each other.

The bridal couple had chosen to forgo a traditional parent dance for the second song, instead making it a blend of couples: Andrew with Mrs. O'Keefe, Jen with her father, and Noah and Lily.

"This is it," Noah said, but Lily heard the tension in his voice. The memory of last night came to her, fresh and beautiful as they walked to the dance floor together. Noah took her hand in his but his body remained stiff. Lily swallowed and stepped a breath closer. "Noah," she whispered.

"What?" He looked down at her, a spare, cold glance that told her how difficult this was for him despite their practice run. Or maybe because of it.

"Dance with me, Noah." She slipped her hand onto his waist and held his gaze. She could feel the warmth of his skin through his crisp shirt and white vest.

His feet began to move and hers followed, her eyes never leaving his. She could tell the moment he started to relax, the moment his hand softened in hers and his rigid posture settled beneath her fingers.

"Thank you for all you've done, Lily."

"I promised, didn't I?"

He smiled a tiny smile. "Yes, you did."

"And I never go back on a promise, remember?"

He moved their joined hands and touched her cheek with a fingertip. "I remember. Even when I tried to force you to."

"Yes well, you should be glad you didn't succeed. I mean, you'd be left without a dancing partner tonight."

"I'd be left without a friend, as well. Even if she is wearing pink."

"How very cruel of you to bring that up, Mr. Laramie," she coquetted.

"I don't know what your issue is with pink, after all. It suits you."

"It goes back to something my mother said once."

Several beats of music passed. "Are you going to enlighten me?" He angled his head, regarding her curiously. "Surely you're not going to leave it at that."

Lily remembered the moment quite clearly. When she'd been crying in the hotel room and Jasmine had been helping her out of the gown. *"Really Lily,"* her mother had said disparagingly. *"White? You had to go for white? Pink suits you so much better. White is so predictable."*

It had hurt her terribly at the time, as if she cared about a dress when all her plans were being washed away like a dirty secret.

"Lil?" His voice was soft now, and she realized there were two tears on her cheeks. Mortified, she sniffed, taking her hand from his back for a moment to hurriedly wipe them away.

"Don't say anything, please," she begged quietly. "Smile and dance. That's all I want from you."

When the song was over, Lily took her hand from his and walked away.

CHAPTER NINE

LILY TOOK SEVERAL DEEP breaths to regain her composure. She'd fought hard against the memories today, but there were times that they sneaked around her defenses so easily. The smell of the flowers, or the step onto the carpet runner. As much as she had told herself she was over it and it didn't matter, she still bore the scars of that awful day.

But she couldn't leave yet, not when there were still traditions to be upheld. The bouquet had yet to be thrown and several more minutes of dancing before the bride and groom would sneak off for a very brief honeymoon. It would be bad form for the maid of honor to leave before the bride and groom. Besides, what explanation could she give? Certainly not that the whole day was a reminder of broken dreams and crushed hopes. And definitely not that her feelings for the best man were getting in the way. The last thing she wanted was for Jen or Andrew to put their hopes in that direction.

Guests now took the floor as the music changed to something with a solid dance beat, and Lily went to the punch bowl, pouring herself a plastic cup of the sweet pink drink to keep her hands occupied. It only took seconds for Noah to be at her side again.

"What just happened?"

She took a sip and focused on the line of dancers on the floor. If she looked at him now he'd know that it was him affecting her. She hadn't quite spoken the truth when she said a dance was all she wanted from him. And yet she was sure she didn't want more than that, either.

The plain truth was that when she was with Noah she didn't know *what* she wanted.

"Nothing."

"Lily."

His hand stopped the progress of her cup and she looked up at him in annoyance as the punch sloshed close to the rim. Sometimes she liked him a whole lot better when he wasn't so clued in. She sighed. "Just let it go, Noah. It doesn't matter."

Noah released her wrist, but didn't move away from her. He'd promised to stick by her side during the wedding, knowing she wasn't looking forward to it any more than he was. But this went beyond a simple promise.

He swallowed, looked down at her profile. She was so beautiful. She'd done something curly and wispy to her hair, tiny pearls shimmering from within the dark strands. Her skin glowed next to the pale pink of the gown, begging to be touched. He reached out and touched her bare shoulder, craving the sight of her eyes locked on his. He wasn't disappointed. At the moment his fingertips grazed her soft skin, her head turned and her gaze clashed with his.

He let his finger trail over her shoulder and down her arm, the touch so light it skimmed over her skin like a soft breath. "What are you doing?" She whispered it and he barely caught the words, but he saw them form on her lips and he smiled.

Seducing you, he thought suddenly, smiling. It sounded ridiculous. They had kissed last night, and today he'd touched her as it had been required. But seduction was something different. Seduction demanded a conclusion. And he knew that was out of the question. No, he wouldn't seduce her, wouldn't let it go too far. There was too much undecided in his life to complicate things further. Too many decisions he was putting off making, weighing him down. But he couldn't seem to stop the simple caress, either.

"I'm touching you. Do you want me to stop?"

"I…"

Her hesitation did wonders for his confidence. He didn't want her to see what was beneath the surface, but knowing that he had the power to make her lose her words, the power to make her sigh into his mouth as they'd kissed… She had run out of his house last night and he'd thought it was because he had gone too far. That he had repulsed her as she'd touched his arm. But now, he saw the top of the strapless bodice of her dress rise and fall with the force of her breath and he knew she was feeling it as strongly as he was.

But they were here, in the Larch Valley Community Center with his brother and new sister-in-law and old friends and his mother in attendance. He scanned the crowd. He saw old schoolmates and local business owners, like Jim Barnes, who still owned Papa's Pizza, and Agnes Dodds, who'd rapped his fingers with a ruler in elementary school and now ran the local antique store. This was no place to broadcast that he lusted after the maid of honor. No, not lusted. Lusted was too superficial, and there was more to Lily than that.

She moved one single finger against his as his hand trailed past her wrist. A brushing of contact that somehow said *no, don't stop*. That said she was feeling it, too.

And for once Noah didn't want to think about the mistakes he'd made, or if his recovery was on schedule, or what choices he'd have to make about how to serve his country. For once he wanted to live in the moment. To think only about the gorgeous woman whose hand was twined with his and whose eyelashes now lay demurely against her cheeks as she avoided looking at him.

"Can I take you home?"

His question was rewarded by her lifting her head, giving him a glimpse of the piercing blue of her irises. "We can't leave yet."

He took a step backward. Perhaps he'd misread.

"But I'd like that. Later."

She smiled up at him, sweetly, and without the edge he was used to seeing. It hit him in the gut with the force of a punch. Noah nodded. "Let me know when you're ready."

To be in each other's pockets now would be too obvious. For one, he was already having a difficult time not touching her. They had to mingle, speak to others rather than gazing into each other's eyes the entire time. He checked his watch. "I'm going to go talk to Clay for a bit," he said to her, finally letting her fingers go. "Enjoy yourself."

He forced himself to leave her there, walking over to where Clay stood at the side of the floor. Talking to him about looking after Lazy L in Andrew's absence wasn't nearly as interesting as spending time with Lily.

But it was the right thing to do.

Once Jen and Andrew had thrown the bouquet and garter and escaped under a shower of rice, Lily made herself busy at the head table, packing wineglasses into a padded box.

"What are you doing?"

She jumped at the sound of his voice, especially when she'd just been thinking of him again. The way he'd touched her earlier had nearly sent her up in flames. Now he was right behind her, so close she could feel the warmth of his body, and her fingers shook as she placed the last of the special wedding glasses in the tissue.

She took a breath and closed the box. "The bride and groom glasses. Jen asked if I'd pick them up."

"Then are you ready to go?"

She bit down on her lip. She shouldn't accept the drive home. Anyone here would give her a lift. She was getting far too involved with Noah.

But as she looked up into his strong, handsome face, she knew it didn't matter. It was Noah that she wanted to be with. It was Noah's humor and understanding that had made today bearable.

And it was Noah she trusted.

"Yes, I'm ready."

There were no more options, no more diversions or prevarications. Lily was going with him. And she was still unsure of what she wanted the night to bring.

They resumed walking, out the double doors to the parking lot. The sound of the dance beat a steady rhythm behind them, a muted thump that seemed incongruous in the otherwise quiet night. It was the time of day Lily loved best, when the light hadn't quite faded from the sky, leaving it a swirl of indigo and lavender and peach, and the first stars poked through the curtain of falling darkness. Their steps slowed as they walked to Noah's truck, making crunching sounds on the gravel.

Conversation would have felt out of place. Noah opened her door and held the box of crystal while she got in. What was between them now was too fragile, too tenuous to spoil with conversation. She had needed him today. She'd needed his steady presence; she'd needed the distraction he provided.

She still needed it.

Noah got in, started the engine and made the short drive to her town house.

As he idled the truck on the street, she knew she didn't want to go in alone. She didn't want to go upstairs and remove her bridesmaid gown with an empty house and a head full of memories for company. She didn't want to face the post-wedding letdown that already felt hollow in her heart. Somewhere along the way she'd started needing him. She'd started trusting him. And the simple truth was that there was no one else she wanted to spend time with tonight. She wanted to be with him, not because he kept her mind off other things, but because the air felt a little bit colder when he wasn't around to warm it. Because he'd touched her in ways she hadn't been touched in a very long time and she wasn't ready for it to end yet.

"Do you want to come in? I can put on some coffee."

She looked over at him, his features highlighted by the colored lights of the dashboard. The tie that had been so precisely knotted earlier was loosened and at a crooked angle against the crisp collar of his shirt. The tuxedo jacket buttons were undone, the inky-black material flowing away from his body as he put the truck in Park. A memory flashed through her mind, of Noah coming out of the change room, looking slightly rumpled. But that image had nothing on the deliciousness of the real thing before her now.

She wasn't prepared to want him this much.

The moment held, tethering them together by some invisible force, until his eyes warmed and he replied, "I'd like that."

The house was dark as Lily fumbled with the keys, unlocking the front door. Once inside, she went to the kitchen, turning on the under-the-counter lighting. Noah followed behind, looking tall and elegantly gorgeous in his tuxedo. Lily's hands shook as she prepared the coffeemaker and flipped the switch. Nerves fluttered through her stomach, over her skin, making her doubt the wisdom of inviting him in. She didn't want to be alone, but being alone with Noah was dangerous, too. This was going further than the physical attraction that kept demanding to be acknowledged. She wanted more. But how much more? Everything? The very thought made her drop the spoon from her hand. In all these years, she'd never been faced with this choice.

She picked up the spoon again and got out the sugar bowl. Maybe it was just the wedding. If she could only convince herself of that! Weddings made people crazy, isn't that what everyone said? She had to break the wedding day spell. The first step would be getting out of the pale pink gown.

"If you don't mind, I'd like to change."

Noah took a step forward, his body blocking her passage. "What if I do mind?"

She swallowed. Tried to be annoyed that he'd stopped her, but a delicious shiver feathered over her, simply in an elemental response to his nearness.

Another step, and he reached out his hand, placing it over the smooth fabric covering her ribs, down over her waist. "You look beautiful."

"Noah…"

But he wasn't deterred, not by the gurgle of the coffee brewing or by her weak protest. His right foot joined his left, leaving only a breath between them. "Beautiful. Like strawberry ice cream." His hand moved up, his finger tracing along the fine stitching and pink crystals at the top of the bodice.

She couldn't breathe, couldn't think.

His mouth descended, toying with hers. "Soft." His kiss was barely a glance on her lips. "And sweet." And his tongue touched her bottom lip, tasting.

She had no defense against his gentle persuasion. Her hand twined with his hair as she drew his head down, kissing him fully, tasting the sweetness of champagne and cake, the tartness of punch and the seductive flavor that was simply Noah.

The passion rose so quickly between them it pulled her breath out of her lungs. His body pressed her backward so that she was bolstered by the kitchen counter, and his hand braced on the granite edge. And still the kiss went on, Lily's head tilted back so that the tips of her hair touched the satin back of her dress. Noah's lips slid from hers and down the column of her neck, gentling as he tasted the skin there before moving back up and pulling her earlobe into his mouth.

It drew a quiet moan from her, and they paused as the sound echoed through the kitchen. And in that soft, prolonged moment, everything caught up with her. This was too much, too fast, too everything. They had to stop. It would only end in heartache, and the ache would be hers.

She let go of the resolve that had held her together throughout the day and everything came flooding back. The chapel in Las Vegas, Curtis, their parents, the hope crushed. And in that moment, she started to cry. Quiet, heart-breaking tears. All she'd ever wanted was a place to belong. A home. And she'd thought she'd found it in Larch Valley.

But Noah had changed that. He'd changed *everything*. The satisfaction she'd built into her life here was no longer enough. And he was offering her no more than a few kisses. It was all he *had* to offer.

"Lily…" His voice was tortured, pulling her close to him. "Lily, don't cry. You *never* cry."

His hand was on the back of her head, tucking her against his shirt that smelled of starch and cologne. No, she never cried. She was always upbeat Lily, who hid those hurts inside. She was tired of being that person. When had she last been able to truly be herself? When was the last time she'd let someone see who she really was?

"What is it?" He whispered the question in her ear, sending shivers down her spine as his breath warmed her hair. "Tell me."

Lily sighed against his shirtfront. How could she possibly explain to him how she had come to care so deeply, in such a short time? That being with him had thrown the rest of her world into flux. "I don't know if I can."

"Does it have something to do with the dress you had on that day?"

"I should have known you'd remember," she whispered, blinking against a new onslaught of tears. She hadn't wanted to tell him about Curtis, but it was far better to do that than probe her feelings for him out loud. "When you saw it and thought it was Jen's…"

"But it wasn't." He rested his chin on the top

of her head, the pressure comforting. "I knew when I saw Jen step onto that runner today. Was it yours?"

She nodded, sniffling. "Yes."

He said nothing more, just held her close for several minutes.

Finally Lily pulled away and looked up into his face. That steady, strong face that had seen so many things during the years. After wars and battles, she knew her past would seem trivial to him. "It seems silly," she whispered, putting a hand against his chest, a flimsy barrier between them. "Look at you, and what you've been through. This is nothing compared to that."

"Everyone has their own crosses to bear. Just because yours is different than mine doesn't make it any less important. Or any less difficult. So are you going to tell me what happened? Was it divorce?"

It was a logical conclusion for him to make. "Oh, Noah, it was such a long time ago."

He smiled then, a soft, indulgent curving of his lips. "And you call me stubborn." He reached down and took her hand, tugging it until she followed him to a chair in the living room. And then he sat, pulling her down with him so she was on his lap, her skirts billowing out around them. Gingerly he settled his right shoulder against the plush upholstery and she wondered if his arm was paining him after the long day. Carefully she leaned toward his left side, her hand circled his neck, and she looked down at him, memorizing each angle and tiny wrinkle. He was beautiful, she realized. Not just on the outside. Inside, too. Obstinate, and sometimes prickly, but that was just a cover.

It would be so easy to fall completely over the edge into love. But perhaps telling him the truth would be enough to put some space between them.

"When I was eighteen, I ran away to be married. His name was Curtis and we had been planning it for months. Just waiting for my birthday so I would be legal. He was in first year university and I was nearly finished high school."

Noah didn't ask questions, just kept his arm solidly around her, stroking her bare arm with his fingers. Sitting there, snuggled up in a chair, Lily felt secure and comforted. Noah wasn't just a good-looking guy she was attracted to. Somehow they'd become friends over the past weeks. Somehow she'd found herself telling him things she hadn't revealed to another living soul. And it felt good to finally tell *someone* about it. She looked into his eyes, the inky color of deep twilight, marveling at the change in her heart. She had never wanted anyone in Larch Valley to find out about her previous mistakes. But it was easier to reach into the past for explanations than to confess her present feelings.

"Curtis saved up his money. His family was a lot better off than we were and so he squirreled away funds to pay for the hotel and the plane tickets. My mom was a dressmaker. I already knew I could sew my own dress, so I bought the material on the sly and designed it."

The hand on her arm stopped moving. "You designed it? The dress you had on? That's amazing."

"I was always drawing new ideas. I made most of my own clothes back then." She realized she hadn't designed anything new in years, and missed the feeling of the pencil in her hand, the way the lines felt as images translated from her head to paper. She sighed. "I lost a lot of my dreams that day, Noah."

She slid farther down on his lap. "We made it

to Vegas. We even made it to the chapel. But when we got to the part about objections, the door opened. And there were Curtis's parents, and my mom."

"Oh, Lily." Noah's voice was soft in the darkness. "They stopped the wedding."

"Legally we could have continued. I was eighteen, an adult. But Curtis's parents, who'd always been good to me…" She swallowed, remembering how she'd felt small and ugly and worthless. "They made it very clear that I wasn't the kind of girl that he should marry. Dating was one thing. I guess they'd never realized how serious we were. I was a nobody. And he was destined for bigger and better things than an unfortunate marriage."

"And what did Curtis say?"

She laughed then, a bitter sound in the dark. "Our plan had been for him to finish school, go into business with his father as agreed. I was going to design, and open a little boutique. Funny how that plan evaporated once his father said if we went through with it he'd be cut off."

"He walked away from you?"

"Without a second's hesitation. Left with his parents and me standing at the altar, so to speak."

"Then he didn't love you."

Lily's heart seemed to sink to her feet. It hurt to hear him state the truth. What did she expect from Noah? Not love, certainly. He would leave, as Curtis had. He would do his duty. And she would be left behind again. No one had ever cared enough to stay. "Oh, I know. Believe me."

"No man who ever loved you could ever walk away."

And just like that her heart soared up, back into her chest again. What was it about Noah that made her feel special? Worth it? She'd never been worth the trouble before.

"What about your mother?"

His question drew her out of the sweetness of the moment. Lily's answering laugh was bitter with cynicism. Her mother had been a real piece of work, too. For a woman so concerned with *feelings*, she had been astonishingly immune to Lily's pain, even as Lily had left the chapel in tears. "Oh, my mom called them a bunch of snobs and then proceeded to tell me it was for the best. I had to endure hours of her saying how I'd been foolish and too young to put my life into one person when I had my whole life ahead of me, full of adventure. I didn't want adventure."

"And so your heart was broken and nobody cared."

"Yes." She whispered it.

"Now I know why you don't like weddings."

"I would never have said anything to Jen. I know it doesn't make sense. They love each other and I'm happy for them. At the same time...Curtis said he loved me, too. And yet it was so easy for him to leave. I'm not sure I believe in love that lasts forever. At least not for me."

She sat up slightly, looking down into his eyes. Now she wondered if Jasmine had somehow been right after all. How much time had she wasted, lamenting old dreams instead of finding new ones? When was the last time she'd let herself have an adventure? Instead she had settled for something else, an imitation of the dream she'd wanted. She had the home she'd always craved, but it felt empty. Look what happened when she finally let go of the rigid control she usually exerted over her life. She was on the brink of being hurt just as much this time as last, and it wasn't worth it.

"My mom always said life was too short to fall in love only once. She called me predictable and small-minded when I said I wanted something other than the life she had."

"Is she happy?"

The question surprised her. Was Jasmine happy? She'd always insisted she was. She'd always seemed like this free spirit that lived in the moment, beautiful. Lovers had come and gone. Some of them had been good to Lily and she'd secretly hoped for a father, but that had never happened. But what about now? Lily didn't know. Other than dutiful cards on birthdays and Christmas, she hadn't spoken to her mother in many years.

And she felt ashamed that she had to answer, "I don't know."

Noah sighed, and Lily asked, "What about your mom? Did she seem happy to you?"

"No. She's spent her whole life looking for happiness and never finding it. Not with my father and certainly not with her second husband. I'm not angry at her anymore. And yet, it's hard to let go when people hurt us. When people we are supposed to be able to count on let us down. Even," he added quietly, "when that person is yourself."

He understood.

"She's not a particularly strong woman, Lily."

His eyes were nearly black in the darkness of the room. "Not like you."

No one had ever called her strong before. Reliable, sure. Ready to do a favor, yes. But no one had ever seen to the core of her the way Noah could. She'd tried to use her past as a barrier to their relationship, expecting him to back away. But instead he'd broken straight through it.

And while it was a relief to finally let down that guard, it was scary. Because Noah, like everyone else she'd cared about, would be leaving, too. What was the alternative? Marriage? She'd be a disaster as an army wife, left home alone while he was deployed. And what about children? How could she subject children to life as army brats, moving from base to base, school to school, knowing how difficult it could be?

She pushed herself off his lap, wiping her fingers beneath her eyes. "I must look awful. I'm going to change. But help yourself to coffee."

Before he could reply, she rushed to the stairs and up to her room.

Noah was not permanent. No more than Jasmine had been or Curtis had been. She had to remember that.

It was just as well that his recovery was well in hand and that there were only a few weeks left until she would be back to work.

Because wishes were pointless, and now that the wedding was over, it was time she started making a break. It would be best for everyone.

CHAPTER TEN

IT HAD BEEN A LONG DAY.

Noah had done the bulk of the chores himself, and it had taken him longer than he liked. Pixie had bumped his right side hard when he'd gone into her stall, and he still felt the ache in his shoulder. And on top of it all, it had been the middle of the night before he'd gotten to sleep. He simply hadn't been firing on all cylinders today.

He'd lain there thinking of Lily, turning what she'd told him over and over in his head, thinking about her and the wedding, and about the army and Lazy L until it all blended together in his head. The result was he'd awakened even more confused.

What did Lily want from him? A friend? More than that? She had confided in him, and he'd encouraged it. He'd never done such a thing in his life. Dating had been a superficial way to put in time, to appease some of the loneliness and longing, but he'd never been in love. There hadn't been time. He'd always kept things light. He'd been careful to keep it casual on both sides, not to create expectations he couldn't fulfill.

But Lily was different.

Now, as he struggled to open a box of pasta, he scowled. She had managed to get past the usual barriers. And last night…last night he'd come very close to forgetting about everything *but* her and how much he'd wanted her.

He ripped at the cardboard, resulting in a nasty paper cut. "Dammit!" He let go of the box, sticking his finger in his mouth, and the package dropped to the floor, scattering bits of rotini all over the kitchen.

He was in a mess, tired, angry, and unable to even put on a Band-Aid. Sometimes it truly felt like two steps forward and then one step back, never advancing as quickly as he wanted. Why did the simplest things have to be so difficult?

"Noah?"

Lily's voice had him swinging toward the door. She stood on the other side of the screen, peering in. He took his finger out of his mouth and watery blood formed around the cut. He grabbed the tea towel from the counter to cover the finger.

"Hang on." There was no time to clean up the mess. He shut off the burner and went to the door.

She wore jeans today, and a copper-colored T-shirt that clung to her curves. Beaded sandals were on her feet. She looked just as attractive this way as she had yesterday in her gown and pearls.

"Lily." He pushed the door open, inviting her in. She stepped inside and reached into her purse.

"You forgot this last night," she said quietly, holding out his tie. He stared at it, remembering how he'd slid it from around his neck as he'd pressed his body against hers.

"The formal wear shop will want it back with the tux." Lily gave the tie a slight shake, drawing him out of the memory.

He reached out to take it, then realized he couldn't. The last thing he should do was get blood on a white tie.

"What have you done?" Lily put the tie on a bookcase and grabbed his hand. She pulled off the tea towel, looking at his finger. "You cut yourself."

"It's just a paper cut. That happens to be bleeding a lot."

She bit down on her lip as she gripped his finger. "Where are your Band-Aids? I'll put one on for you."

"I'll do it myself." He pulled his hand away, feeling like a child. "The stuff I take to keep the swelling down makes my blood a little thinner, that's all."

He spun away, heading for the bathroom. He didn't need her to do every little thing for him. Good lord, he could care for himself! He found the kit beneath the sink and flipped it open, using his teeth to tear a bandage from a perforated strip. He ripped it open—again using his teeth—and tried to wrap it around the finger.

The plastic wrinkled and stuck to itself. He reached for a replacement, ripping too hard and destroying another Band-Aid.

He swore, then leaned against the sink, breathing heavily.

Last night he'd felt like a normal man. Last night his decision had made sense, and he'd felt as if he could handle anything. And he'd known that a life behind a desk, stuck within four walls was not the kind of life for him. But today he couldn't even put on a Band-Aid. Now Lily was here, looking as pretty as ever, and the last thing he wanted to do was disappoint her. She'd had too many disappointments.

What a mess. If he backed away now he knew how it would look to her. As though what she'd told him about her past made a difference. And to let things go forward would be a mistake. Where could they possibly go? He certainly couldn't love her the way she wanted. The way she deserved.

"Noah?"

He spun around as her voice startled him, and smacked his injured arm spectacularly on the door frame.

White-hot pain radiated through his stump, nearly bringing him to his knees as he caught his breath. Lily, the feminine, beautiful Lily, cursed in alarm as he started to slip, then slid beneath his left arm, bolstering his weight.

"Come sit down," she said, urging him toward the dining area and pulling out a chair. He sank into it, closing his eyes and baring his teeth to keep from crying out. It wasn't just the stub. It was his entire arm, right down to the fingertips that were no longer there.

Phantom pain. Now and again it struck, some-times after a bump or for no particular reason at all. Today, when he was especially tired, it had been worse than usual, flashing off and on, tingling. But now it was a searing line that took his breath away.

"Oh, Noah. What can I do?" Lily's panicked voice came from his right and he forced his eyes open. Her bright blue gaze was focused on his face, guilt on each delicate feature.

"It's not your fault. It's been a long day. And I wasn't watching where I was going."

Cold sweat beaded on his forehead. This was not how he wanted it. He wanted to keep this part of it hidden from her. The part of his injury that reduced him to a quivering mess. Most of the time he coped. But there were times it took him unawares, and all he could do was wait it out. Times when he was tired, or stressed, or if he simply overexerted himself. A frustration and a symptom to be expected, the doctors said. Listen to your body, they said.

If only it were that easy. Right now his body was screaming at him.

"Is there medication I can get you?"

He shook his head. The over-the-counter stuff was useless.

He looked up at her, recognizing the expression of helplessness on her face. Lord knew, he'd felt that way often enough when he'd seen his soldiers get wounded and had been unable to make it right. Speaking to them at the airfield as they were being patched up. Or as they were being prepped for transport to Germany. He hated that the boot was on the other foot now.

Icy-hot daggers shot down his arm and he gritted his teeth. She had trusted him with the story of Curtis. Could he trust her, as well, to see the scar he bore?

"Can we ice it or something? There must be some way to help," she insisted.

He caught his breath as the muscles spasmed in protest. At some point, someone was going to see his stump without its protective covering. As the muscles seized, he knew he needed to do something to help the pain, and that of anyone, Lily would be the most practical nurse.

"Heat relaxes the muscles. There's a pack in the medicine cupboard."

As she left to retrieve it, he tried to roll up his sleeve. But it had rained this morning and he'd put on a long-sleeved cotton shirt, making the chore even more challenging. When Lily came back, she put the pack on the floor and unpinned his cuff.

"Roll it up," he said.

She tried, but there was too much fabric and the roll was too tight over the muscles that corded just below his shoulder.

"You've got to take it off," she said.

The stabbing pain continued and he breathed through gritted teeth. "No."

"Yes." She went in front of him and began working the buttons.

"Lily, no," he said weakly, as she slipped each button from its hole, unable to fight her beyond putting his left hand over her wrist, stopping her movements. He didn't want her to see him this way. It was too ugly.… It would be a sight she would remember each time she looked at him. A man covered in ugly scars. Not the Noah who had danced with her in the dark.

But she pushed his hand away and kept on until the last button was undone and she spread the sides wide to ease it off his shoulders.

Then she saw.

And she cried out, the sound filled with the shock of the sight before her.

He knew what she was seeing right now. The angry red marks, the puckered scars of the cuts caused by the shrapnel. A beast.

"Oh, Noah...I didn't know." Her breath hitched with emotion. "Why didn't you tell me?"

"I didn't want you to see," he whispered, turning his head away.

Noah wasn't a man who wept. He hadn't cried in the hospital, or when he'd gone to his father's grave site, or when he'd seen his mother for the first time in over two decades. But at this moment, he was unable to stop the tears from coming as Lily stood back, covering her mouth and staring at the vision before her. The tears formed, hot and bitter, sliding over his lower lashes when he blinked.

Lily gaped at the sight of his battered skin. My God, the pain he must have gone through. Not just the arm, but several red scars from his chest to his abdomen. She looked into his face. Noah was crying. *Crying.* The sight nearly undid her, seeing the pain and shame on his face. But he shouldn't be ashamed. He had done nothing wrong, nothing to deserve the cuts that marred his body.

They did not define him. Not to her. To her they were medals, badges of his strength, his dedication, his sacrifice.

Lily sniffed, wiped at the tears on her cheeks, and saying nothing, stepped forward, easing him out of the shirt, taking it and laying it gently over another chair. Questions flooded her mind about what had really happened to him, questions she was afraid to ask amid the profound sympathy she felt, not only for his injuries but because it was clear to her that the marks they left behind caused him a deeper pain that hadn't yet begun to heal. Not all of his scars were on the outside, she realized. They had left their mark on his soul, as well. And that was something she could understand very well.

"What can I do to help you?"

He swallowed. Reached over and removed the shrinker covering the stump, revealing the entire wound to her eyes for the first time. She bit down on her lip at the sight, at the supreme trust that the gesture meant. She remembered dancing with him and his whispered words of wanting to be perfect for her. And he was, in many ways, naked before her now. His trust in her was the most humbling experience of her life.

"Just give me the pack," he said, taking it from her hands. He anchored one side in his armpit, then wrapped it around, feeling the warmth seep into the muscles, relaxing them and easing the spasms.

She moved a chair closer to him, sitting on it. And then she covered his fingers with her own, holding the pack in place.

"I had no idea, Noah." She said the words gently, needing to acknowledge what she'd seen and show him it didn't matter.

"You weren't supposed to," he replied, his chin jutting out defiantly. "No one was."

"Why?"

He turned his head and stared into her eyes, a mixture of pain and defiance in his gaze.

"Why do you think? It's ugly. I'm a mess of scars and incisions. No one should have to look at me this way," he said, turning his head away. "What woman would want a man like this?"

In that moment, Lily bled for him. He had always seemed so sure of himself. Yes, he'd had challenges, but he'd always been so determined to move forward. How could she have missed it? Of course his self-image would have suffered. He'd done a good job of hiding it, but not tonight. Tonight she was seeing it all. And what she saw was a man not defined by his scars but by the strength of his heart.

"Did you think I would be repulsed?"

"Aren't you?"

"Absolutely not."

The words settled around them. Had she been shocked, seeing the extent of his wounds? Yes. It had been unexpected. But repulsed? Not in the least. Her only thought had been of the pain he must have endured.

Lily eased the pack off his stump. "What else can I do?"

Noah didn't reply, so Lily stood, cupped his chin in her fingers and lifted it so he was looking into her face. Then she touched her forehead to his, closing her eyes. His body stiffened; she knew he was fighting her but she was determined to wait.

"What can I do, Noah?" Her voice was barely a whisper, but she heard him swallow. She framed his face with her hands, touching her lips to his, carefully, lightly. Trying not to cry. The time would come to cry later. Right now he was in pain. How long had he been toughing this out alone?

"Massage helps."

Without a moment's hesitation, Lily went to

his side and began kneading the muscles. The flesh was strong and firm beneath her fingers, and she marveled at the sight of the scar tissue and shape of the tip as she worked from his shoulder down his bicep. Noah closed his eyes and she felt the tension seep out of him as she pressed and kneaded gently.

Shadows fell in the room as the sun moved around toward the west side of the house. Lily's hands slowed, moved beyond his right arm to the back of his neck, working the warm, smooth skin beneath her fingers. Touching him the way she'd wanted to for weeks now. Learning the shape of him, the hardness of his body from the life he'd led. Flawed, but beautiful. She massaged his other shoulder, the one that now bore the brunt of all his daily tasks, and down his left arm until she was in front of him again. He stood up from his chair and reached for his shirt, holding it loosely in his fingers.

He would have put it on but Lily stayed his arm with her hand.

"Don't. Not yet."

She reached out a fingertip and touched each scar, each angry red ridge of tissue. She bit down on her lip as she explored, feeling a reverence she hadn't expected. What sort of man suffered such an injury and returned so strong, so determined? Each scar made him more of a man in her eyes, not less. The love she'd felt before was nothing compared to the feeling swelling her heart right now.

"How did you get these?" she asked finally, looking up.

"The explosion that took off my arm also sent little pieces of shrapnel everywhere. I got peppered."

What atrocities had he seen? She could only imagine what it had been like in the theater of battle. "You've never said much about that day."

"What was the point?" His voice was quiet, husky. "It was early in the morning, before dawn. Things had been quiet for days. It happened so fast, and I was asleep. I pulled on my combats and grabbed my rifle. Three of my men were pinned down. I went in to help. Then the grenade went off. I hadn't put on my vest."

A muscle pulsed in his jaw. "It was a stupid mistake, careless. I knew better. I was an officer, for God's sake. Not some green kid on their first deployment."

Lily could see it playing out in her head and

suddenly things became clearer. Did Noah blame himself for making a mistake? She hated that he doubted himself for even a second. He was only human. "And the men?"

"Finished their deployment safe and sound. I think they made it home ahead of me, actually."

"So you saved them."

Her hands rested on his chest, feeling the rise and fall of his breathing, the beating of his heart that accelerated beneath her touch. He'd sacrificed himself. And the fact that her hands on his skin seemed to cause his body to respond sent a thrill through her.

"No. I screwed up and got lucky," he murmured.

"Would it have changed anything? If you'd had it on?"

He was silent for a long moment. "I suppose not. It wouldn't have saved my arm. But I still have to live with the marks, always reminding me, you know?"

She leaned forward the slightest bit and pressed her lips to one of the scars, closing her eyes and wishing she could make it go away.

"You don't have to pretend, Lily." He quivered beneath her lips and hands. "I saw your face."

"I am not pretending anything." She lifted her

face to him, determined he know the truth. Knowing he *deserved* the truth. "Whatever you think you saw, you're wrong. I am not disgusted, Noah Laramie." She swallowed thickly, overwhelmed by her emotions. "I am in awe."

"In awe?" He cleared his throat, stepping away from her a little, his lips dropping open in surprise. "Don't be ridiculous."

But she nodded, surprised at the soft sound of her voice as she spoke the absolute truth—in a way she had never spoken to another man before. "I *am* in awe of you. Of your strength, and your courage, and your compassion. It hurts me to know you think so little of yourself that you hid from me. You never have to hide from me, Noah. Don't you know that now?"

She reached out and ran her fingers over the rough skin, heard his sharp intake of breath and smiled softly. "You're beautiful, Noah."

"Lily…"

The lump in her throat grew until she could hardly speak. "You're beautiful to me," she whispered. And held her breath, knowing that he was everything she hadn't wanted. And that despite it she wanted him more than she wanted breath. More than she'd wanted anything in her entire life.

Noah wrapped his arm around her, tucking her head against his shoulder. How had this happened? He was in love with her. He'd never been in love with anyone in his life. He'd never wanted to be. And she'd blustered her way in with her pragmatic ways. Lily had never said a single word she hadn't meant. So he knew she meant what she said now.

And it was just his luck that when he finally fell into something so impractical, he had no idea where his life was going. The well-ordered path he'd set for himself was gone, obliterated in the dust of his injury.

"I love you, Lily."

Where the words came from, he had no idea. But they fell off his lips like a blessing.

Lily stepped out of his embrace and stared at him, her eyes wide. But not with pleasure, he noted bitterly, absorbing the unexpected hit. Her eyes were wide with dismay and denial, and he wondered if he'd been wrong about her always telling the truth. Had she only said what she had to make him feel better?

Was she capable of that? He couldn't, wouldn't believe that of her.

"You can't love me." Her voice was a harsh rasp in the quiet room as she shook her head.

He clenched his teeth together, disappointed that the one time in his life he'd said those three words to any woman they were not reflected back. "I can love you. And I do. But whether or not you accept it is up to you." The words came out cold, flat, as she stepped away from him.

This was why he'd never gone in for the whole relationship and feelings thing. In the army, he knew what was expected of him, and what he'd get in return. Love was another matter. It was fickle and unpredictable. Like right now.

"If you're better, I should go." Lily's face was pale now, as she skirted around him to retrieve her purse. He marveled at how something so intense could change a hundred and eighty degrees in the blink of an eye. Moments later she went out the door.

He let her go.

He had let himself get caught up in the moment, and he'd shown his hand. You couldn't force someone to love you. And you couldn't force someone to stay. Gerald's and Julie's failures had taught him that.

He'd been a fool to think, even for a moment, that this would be any different.

CHAPTER ELEVEN

LILY STARED AT THE RAIN dripping down the kitchen window. She stirred the hot chocolate in her mug, sipping the rich drink occasionally when the thought occurred. The remnants of a batch of chocolate chip cookies sat in a tin. She felt slightly ill and pushed the container away.

Noah had said he loved her.

She braced her forehead on the back of her hand. What a horrible mess. He wasn't supposed to have feelings. She was supposed to be the one with feelings, and they were supposed to be curable. She had been so certain it had only been a few kisses and friendship on his part. But not love. What kind of future could they have?

Noah was already married. To the army. She'd known it from the beginning. Each day she realized it more. When she saw him recovering. Heard him talking. As her own feelings had deepened, it had been her comfort, her protection. He couldn't have two loves, and she knew his first love was always the service.

Until two days ago. When she saw his scars and realized how truly and deeply she'd fallen.

When the doorbell rang she jumped, sloshing chocolate over the side of the mug and onto the tablecloth. Perhaps it was Jen. She and Andrew had only gone to Montana for a few days of privacy as a honeymoon. The bell sounded again and Lily got up, hoping Jen didn't ask any questions about why she was in flannel pyjama pants and a T-shirt on a rainy afternoon. She didn't want anyone to know that she was in a funk over a man.

Not just any man. Her best friend's new brother-in-law. A man who was only in their lives during a pit stop in his career.

But it was Noah on her step when she opened the door, standing under the eaves in full dress uniform. The rain dripped in a steady beat behind him, and Lily paused, momentarily stunned by the sight of him. The soldier, with the proud and tall bearing, his beret creased precisely over his short, dark hair. And there were medals over his heart.

A whole new Noah she hadn't imagined.

"Can I come in?"

Dumbly she stood aside, opening the door so

he could enter. What was he doing here? In a second of brief panic, she thought he was going to announce he was leaving. But it wasn't time yet, was it? Could it be?

Had he come to say goodbye? She certainly hadn't given him any reason to stay....

As Lily shut the door, Noah held out his hand. In it was a bouquet of sweet peas, deep pink and purple. "No lilies," he said quietly. "And no light pink."

Lily stared at the blossoms as she took them from his hands. How had he remembered what she'd carried in her bridesmaid bouquet? She was touched by the sentiment despite herself. "I'll put these in water," she replied, trying a tentative smile.

Noah reached up and removed his beret, holding it in his hand. His gaze fell on Lily, soft with concern. "Are you feeling okay?"

Lily felt her cheeks bloom. She was in flannel sleep pants and a blue T-shirt, and her hair was in a messy ponytail with bits coming out of it. She looked a fright. Not a bit of makeup graced her face. And she was sure her eyes had dark circles beneath them as she hadn't been sleeping well, either. The last thing she wanted was for him to guess the truth—that she was moping over him. "I'm fine. Just lazy on a rainy day, that's all."

"You're sure?"

"I'm sure."

She went down the hall to the kitchen in search of a vase while Noah took off his boots. She took advantage of the few extra moments to put away the tin of cookies and roll the chocolate-soiled tablecloth into a ball, tossing it into the laundry room. As his footsteps came closer to the kitchen, she hurriedly pulled out her scrunchie and twisted her hair around, forming a coil and anchoring it with the elastic.

He stood at the entrance to the room, and she wished, if he were going to say goodbye, he would just do it and get it over with.

"You're in your uniform." Immediately she felt foolish for stating the obvious, but a small smile curved his lips slightly.

"And you're in your pyjamas."

He stepped forward, moving to stand before her so that she had to tilt her head back to see his face. She had promised herself that she would keep her distance. But now, looking up into his face, it almost felt as though she was begging for his kiss. Which wasn't too far from the truth.

His thumb touched the corner of her mouth. "And you've got a bit of chocolate right here."

The spot burned where he touched, and her lips fell open as her chest cramped. Desire began its insistent throb, and she grabbed onto the word *chocolate* to try to distract herself from the way his hand felt against her skin. "I made cookies," she breathed. "Would you like one?"

"No, thank you."

The pause filled out, growing with unsaid words until Lily could stand no more. What was he doing here? Why was he in his uniform? Was this the end? If so, why wasn't she feeling relief? Why did the thought of him going back to his life leave her with an empty hole of dread in the pit of her stomach?

"Where have you been, all dressed up?"

"A funeral in Drumheller."

The lightbulb flashed on in Lily's mind. "The soldier from the news the other day."

He nodded.

It had been in the papers and on the television the day of the rehearsal, she remembered. But he had said nothing to her about it, and she had assumed he did not know the young corporal who had been killed. But that wasn't the case at all. She realized he'd kept her out of that side of his life completely. The same way he'd hidden his scars from her.

"But you didn't say anything at the wedding."

"What would have been the point?"

"But you knew him?"

"He was in second battalion. I'm a captain in the regiment. It was my duty to go since I was able."

A captain in the regiment. Clearly, he had been motivated by duty—the same duty that would take him back to the forces. Lily was suddenly grateful she hadn't echoed Noah's sentiments back at him the other night. She'd been so tempted. The words had been there, right on the tip of her tongue, scaring her to death. It would only have made everything more difficult, though, in the end. And watching him go away was going to be hard enough.

And yet she couldn't find it within herself to be bitter about it. Noah was different from Curtis, or the father she'd never known. If he left, it was for the right reasons, not because he was weak. No, it was just the opposite. It was his strength, his convictions that would take him away. He'd never once pretended otherwise.

"I'm sorry," she murmured, turning away and picking up her mug of now-cold chocolate. She dumped it down the sink and ran water to rinse out the mug. "It must have been difficult for you."

"It's always difficult. Worse for the families, though."

And that, Lily reasoned, was exactly why she had to let him go. Easier to lose him now, after a few weeks. Because she knew Noah would never be happy unless he was in the thick of things. The army was his Big Adventure. And she couldn't bear being the one left behind. It was a world he chose not to share with her. In all the weeks they'd known each other, she'd never even seen his uniform until today. He'd shut her out of that part of his life. Maybe he had said he loved her, maybe he'd even thought he meant it.

But loving someone meant sharing. And he had never asked her to share in his world.

Nor had he asked for Lily to share hers.

"Why don't you come in and sit down?" She led the way to the living room and sat in a single chair, leaving the sofa for him. Sitting beside him would be too tempting. She would want to touch him. To sit close by him. She would lose her resolve, her perspective, if she let him too close. At least in the single armchair she had some level of protection from his touch, had a hope of remaining logical.

He perched on the edge of the sofa, placing his beret on his knee and toying with the edge. In the silence, she realized he looked exactly as she pictured officers would look when they were about to deliver bad news. Irritation flared. She wished he would just get on with it. But despite her sloppy appearance, she wanted him to see her composed, so she locked the annoyance away and prayed for calm.

"I haven't seen you in uniform before." She folded her hands atop her knee. "Does it feel good to be back in it again?"

Noah wrinkled his eyebrows, as if she was a puzzle he was trying to solve. "A little. Lily I came here to—"

"You've made such great improvement." She cut him off, forcing a smile. She didn't want to hear the words yet. "I bet you can't wait to get back to the service now that the wedding is over and you're healing so well."

Noah's chin flattened and he straightened his back. Whatever he'd started to say was gone, she realized.

"Yes, the doctor said I'll be getting my prosthetic soon."

"That's wonderful." She tried to picture him with an artificial limb, but it wouldn't gel. No, to her he'd always be Noah in faded jeans and a pair of dusty cowboy boots with his shirtsleeve pinned up. That was her Noah. Not this stranger in a pressed and precise uniform. She didn't know how to speak to this man, so official and somber. "Have you found out when you go back to work?"

Again his expression was impossible to read. It amazed her how he could do that. There had been so many times she'd seen his feelings and thoughts so clearly, and yet other times when he was able to close himself off. She held her breath waiting for the answer, hating how awkward and heavy the air felt in the room.

"Anxious to get rid of me?" He raised one eyebrow coolly.

If only it were that simple. She laughed lightly, without her heart being in it. Anxious for him to leave? Never. But needing for it to happen so she could move on? Absolutely. "You've made a point of letting everyone know these few months were just a stop in the road. The army is your life."

"It has been, yes."

"So what now? You said before you'd have to talk to someone about what role your service would take, right?"

Noah got up off the sofa abruptly and went to the fireplace, his back to her. Lily's heart stuttered, struck by the clean, starched lines of his uniform, the gold stripes on his sleeve standing out in bright relief from the dark green. She needed him to just make the break, to walk away as she knew he would. He seemed a stranger to her now, and she missed his grumpiness almost as much as she missed how easily he'd smiled the past few weeks. That man was gone. Perhaps the one before her now was the man he'd been all along. Maybe this was the real Noah and she'd fallen for a fantasy.

"I have some options," he replied. Then he turned, tucking his beret beneath his right arm, close to his body. "Lily, about what I said the other night…"

"You don't have to explain." She tried to make

the smile sincere, but couldn't, not when it hurt just to see him again. "It was a rough night. I understand."

His lips thinned. "You think I didn't mean it?"

The last thing she wanted was for him to take back the words. The only thing that would be worse would be hearing him pretend to mean them. He couldn't, not really. It occurred to her that she didn't know him nearly as well as she thought she did.

"You were hurting. And it was very emotional, Noah. For both of us. This whole time has been, don't you think?" It certainly had been for her. She hadn't planned on falling in love with him, either. But looking at him only reinforced her decision. She could not be an army wife. She wasn't the kind of woman who could keep the home fires burning and be happy. She wasn't the kind of woman who could handle a husband keeping a major part of his life separate from hers. She needed total commitment. She needed to feel like a part of his world, not an appendage to it. She had spent too many years tagging along at the mercy of her mother's life to do it again.

And he needed someone who could stand behind him. She wasn't sure she could be that strong. Not and still be happy. She would hate being the one left behind, wondering where he was, feeling alone. She knew it as surely as she was breathing. And whatever feelings they had, even if it was love—would be poisoned by it.

"I've done nothing but think since you left. About you, about the army, about life…"

"Noah…" She stood, unsure of where he was going, but getting a bad feeling that she wasn't going to like what was coming next.

He stepped forward and grabbed her hand, squeezing her fingers. "I meant what I said, Lily. I love you. I certainly didn't expect it or want it, but I won't pretend otherwise, either." He lifted her fingers and pressed them to his cheek. She fought against wanting to believe him and needing to remain objective. He loved her despite himself. She needed more. She needed everything. Even when she doubted everything even existed.

"You have always been honest with me, from the first day when you told me to stop being a baby and accept some help. I can never repay you for all you've done. Never."

She slipped her hand off his cheek, touched beyond words but with a frisson of fear at hearing him declare his love again. A love out of gratitude? It felt hollow, false. "I don't want you to feel obligated."

"It has nothing to do with obligation, Lily, don't you see?" He refused to give up. "I know it's sudden, but you...the things you said, the way you touched me when you saw my scars...Lily, that was extraordinary. You are extraordinary. I understand that you are afraid. But I don't want to let you go."

She blinked, feeling as if held hostage by her own love, responsible for his feelings and terrified of meeting him halfway. He had been through so much, and she had been there for him. She'd wanted to be. But was it enough to base a life together on? She already knew the answer.

He took her hand again. "Will you marry me, Lily?"

Lily felt none of the excitement that should accompany such a proposal. All she felt was dread and disappointment and a very real fear of what her answer must be. The deep blue of his eyes was bright with hope, the touch of his hand on hers earnest and true. But what would her life become? She'd made her home here. She was happy, wasn't she? And with Noah, she would have to move. Give up her job, a job she loved. And even if he didn't travel for work or go overseas, there would be changes in posting and having to start all over again. A new job, new people, each time withdrawing further into herself. He would have his life in the army. And she would be invisible.

"I can't." And she pulled her fingers out of his and walked away to the kitchen, trying to put some space between herself and his imploring eyes. For a beautiful, flashing moment she had a vision of what it would be like to be his wife. Wasn't being the wife of a soldier better than being without Noah? But that moment was fantasy, not reality. She had made herself a family here. The only family she'd ever known. And a soldier's life held no guarantees. His scars bore the proof of that.

She paused by the kitchen table and put her hands over her face for a few moments, trying to compose herself. Noah still stood in the middle of her living room, and when she turned back to face him he looked as if he'd been struck. Why couldn't they have just kept it light, and been friends as they'd said all along? Why did love have to get involved and ruin everything? She closed her eyes, remembering the look of anguish on his face as his scars had been bared to her. She had wanted him to realize that those scars didn't matter, that they didn't make him less of a man. She had wanted to help, give him strength. But love meant more than that. Love meant thinking of the other person first.

She swallowed, the sight of him looking so strong and tall in his uniform branded on her mind. It had been easy to forget when he'd been working at the ranch. But she knew in her heart the army would always come first for Noah. How could she ask him to stay? He would resent her for making that demand, the same as she knew she would come to resent him if he asked her to leave behind the life she'd built.

She opened her eyes, and said the words she knew she must, even though it was tearing her apart.

"Noah, I'm sorry. But this is for the best. I would not make you happy. I'm sure of it."

His eyes iced over and his jaw tightened, covering the hurt she'd glimpsed. He stared at her a long time, until she looked down at her feet, feeling his censure.

"You are not the woman I thought," he replied, his deep voice rife with disappointment, the words cutting through her like a blade. He put the beret back on his head, using his hand to angle it precisely. As he went to the door, Lily started to follow, but his harsh words stopped her.

"Don't worry. I'll show myself out."

When he'd arrived, she'd expected him to announce his leaving, and he was. But she hadn't thought it would be this way, with anger and hostility. A few minutes later the front door shut quietly, a click rather than a bang. But that click held as much condemnation as any words might have.

Noah's decision had been made, and Lily's response did nothing to change it.

He leaned on the fence, watching the mare Beautiful and the filly, Gorgeous. Silly, feminine names, both of them, and yet they suited. He reached up, tilting the brim of his hat down against the noonday sun. This was home now. These fields where he'd grown up, this stable filled with horses once more. The wide-open space and sunshine and peace and quiet.

Andrew sauntered up, giving Noah a clap on the back and then joining him at the fence.

Married life clearly suited his brother, Noah realized. There was an air of contentment surrounding him that Noah had never seen before. It was as if he was exactly where he belonged and satisfied with it.

The only time Noah had felt more out of place was when he'd stepped off the plane, seeing his brother for the first time in several years.

He'd handled things all wrong with Lily. He should have told her the truth. Made her understand. That had been his plan but it had gone all wrong. He knew the battles she'd fought. She needed a home, a place to belong. Her mother had hauled her from pillar to post during her childhood. He knew how she felt about Larch Valley. But dammit, he had enough pride that he'd wanted her to choose him *for him*. Not because of a decision he'd made. So he'd kept quiet and watched the relationship crumble around them. Maybe she did love him. Just not enough.

The filly cavorted through the paddock, making him smile and drawing him out of his dark thoughts. He gave a nod in her direction. "She looks good, doesn't she?"

"Sure does."

Andrew reached down and plucked a strand of timothy that grew next to the fence post, began chewing on the end. "You're sure this is what you want?"

Noah nodded. He'd thought long and hard lately. He couldn't go back to the life he'd had. It was physically impossible. And he'd discovered the alternative wasn't what he wanted, either. It was time he came home, and stopped avoiding all the things that had kept him away. He just hadn't planned on doing it alone.

"I'm sure."

Andrew's wide grin split his face. "Good. That's real good, bro."

Noah laughed. "You say that now, but I'm used to being the one giving the orders, little brother."

"There's no one I'd rather be partners with. Let's go tell Jen. She's got some lunch ready, too."

As they walked to the house, Noah wondered what Lily was doing on a Sunday afternoon. He'd had plenty of hours to mull things over since leaving her town house, to think about what had happened. The sunshine and fresh air and physical labor had helped clear his mind. And the one thing he had figured out was that he hadn't imagined her feelings. Lily was easy to read. She wasn't capable of being false or manipulative.

And the way she'd responded to his kiss had been genuine. The trembling touch on each of his scars, the waver in her voice when she'd said he was beautiful…that wasn't for show.

The only conclusion he could reasonably come to was that she was scared to death.

Either way, he'd decided to leave the army before he'd ever proposed, and come what may, he was happy with that decision. He'd been as guilty as Andrew of running away from home. The army had filled the gap for years. Now it was time to let go of old resentments and be back where he belonged. With his family. He and Andrew were partners in Lazy L now, and it was a decision that simply felt *good*.

And now, being in Larch Valley on a permanent basis meant he could put his energies into fighting for Lily. Because she expected him to give up. She expected him to walk away just as Curtis had.

And that was the last thing he intended to do.

CHAPTER TWELVE

JEN WAS ELATED AT THE NEWS and gave Noah a gigantic hug, and then proceeded to lay out a lunch of soup and sandwiches. The three of them were just sitting down, talking about plans for the ranch, when the sound of an engine broke through the chatter. Jen stood up and went to the window, looked at Noah, and back to the door. "It's Lily."

Noah's insides twisted and the bite of sandwich in his mouth turned dry. He hadn't seen Lily since the day she'd turned down his proposal. He'd planned on seeing her again when they could be alone. Talk. Not with an audience who knew nothing of what had truly transpired between them.

"Lily, come on in. We were just having lunch. Do you want some? There's plenty."

Lily stepped over the threshold and froze as she saw him, her expression a blend of surprise and awkwardness. He looked down, missing how she used to look at him with welcome in her eyes. Noah forced himself to swallow the bread and sliced turkey before lifting his head to acknowledge her. "Lily," he said quietly.

Lily jerked her head away and smiled at Jen. "I can't stay. I just wanted to drop off the stuff from the reception." She handed over a box. Noah noticed her hand was shaking the tiniest bit. Had she been anxious to get rid of Jen's things? Were they a reminder of how things had gone so wrong between them?

"Thanks, Lil. I appreciate you bringing them over."

A moment of silence fell, filled with awkwardness. Noah watched as Lily pasted on a smile. He knew it was forced, and that it was made worse by his being there.

"It's okay. It's just your flutes and the centerpiece from our table. A few other things I thought you might like to have as keepsakes."

Andrew hopped up from the table to take the box. "I'll put it upstairs," he volunteered.

"I thought you'd both like to know that Lucy had her baby this morning," she added.

Noah watched Lily's face carefully. Color swept

into her cheeks as she avoided his gaze. He remembered her saying once that marriage and children weren't in the cards for her. For a moment he imagined how beautiful she'd be carrying a child. His child. The image was stunning.

"Oh! Boy or girl?"

"A little boy, Alexander. I ran into Brody at the café this morning. He's one proud papa."

"A boy." Jen beamed at Andrew. "There'll be no living with him now, will there. And named after Lucy's father."

"As the first Navarro grandchild should be." Andrew laughed.

Noah pushed back his chair and gathered up his plate and bowl, taking them to the sink. Andrew and Jen, Brody and Lucy…everything was fitting into place in their worlds. But not in his. He was satisfied he'd made the right decision, leaving the army, but it didn't quite work without Lily.

"I'll let you ladies catch up," he said, his voice low. Without saying another word to Lily, he slid past her and out the door. He wouldn't torture her further by being in the way here. But it wasn't over. He'd find a way to fight for her.

* * *

Lily watched him go with sadness in her heart. The little looks they used to exchange, the warm smile he often greeted her with was gone. She hadn't expected to see him here, not on a Sunday. It had been difficult staying away, though she knew it was for the best.

But his reaction to seeing her today left her feeling even more down, if that were possible. She knew it was too much to expect he would be the same smiling Noah after what had happened between them. Feeling awkward was understandable. As Jen and Andrew talked about baby Alexander and made plans to visit Lucy, Lily slipped out the door. Somehow they had to make things right. She would feel awful if the last words they had were angry ones. It wasn't what she wanted him to take back with him, wherever that was going to be.

She found him in the barn, in the tack room tidying the already neat shelves. She stood quietly in the doorway, watching his movements. "Noah?"

He sighed, put down the bridle in his hand and turned. No smile, no welcoming warmth in his eyes. "What can I do for you, Lily?"

His brusqueness made words catch in her

throat before she could set them free. "You could stop hating me, for starters."

She saw his throat bob as he swallowed. The tension in his eyes softened the slightest bit. "I don't hate you."

"I'm glad. Because I don't like how we left things. We were friends, first. I want to be that again." She didn't want this to be the pattern in her life. She and Curtis had never seen each other again after it had gone wrong. Noah was too important to lose altogether. Somehow they had to make things right, not marked by bitterness and regret.

"I don't know." He picked up the bridle again and went to hang it on its proper hook.

"Noah, when you go back to the service, I don't want it to be with anger at me. Maybe that's selfish. But we shared a lot more than just those last few days. That's what I'd like you to remember. Not how it ended."

He gave up any pretense of working and sat on a sawhorse, his long legs stretched out in front of him.

"I'm not going back."

"Not going back… What do you mean?" Lily felt the color leach from her face. But his uniform the other day…and the way he'd spoken… Her knees wobbled as her emotions reeled. Did this mean he wasn't leaving? That he would be here in Larch Valley? For a brief moment she rejoiced. Then she remembered she had turned him away. She had been the one to refuse.

Had he actually said the words at her house? Or had she simply assumed by his appearance that he was being taken off his temporary status? Had he been let go because of his disability?

Once again, she didn't know the answers. He hadn't let her in. Once again, he hadn't trusted her. She tasted the bitterness of futility in her mouth.

"I applied for a voluntary discharge. I'm not going back into the army. I'm going into partnership with Andrew instead. Trading in my stripes for cowboy boots."

The light was dim in the tack room, but Lily could see enough to know he was completely serious. "But…but…" she stammered. The army was everything to him. He'd said so. There had never been any doubt. "When you came to the house the other day…"

"You made it very clear my proposal was unwelcome."

His steady regard sent her nerve endings skittering. "You had on your uniform," she insisted.

"I had been to a funeral."

"And you never said…you never mentioned you were even considering this!" She backed up slightly, leaning against the doorjamb, letting it support her. That was the trouble, wasn't it. He *never* said. He kept her in the dark.

His smile was small, cold. "Why does it matter? I'd made my decision before then anyway."

Leaving the army, putting his life as a soldier behind him for good? It didn't make sense. His whole identity was wrapped up in being a soldier.

"Why? The army is everything to you. You told me it was your *home*." She took a step inside the room, putting her hands in her jeans pockets. She was so tempted to go to him, and knew she must not.

"The army made up for a lot of things that were missing in my life. For a lot of years, it was my family. But in the end, I knew I'd only be going back in an administrative role." He waved his hand, encompassing the tack room. "I can't be shut up in an office, Lily. I would be grossly unhappy. I need to be outdoors. Where there is room to breathe. I wouldn't be able to go back and be with my men again. And Andrew's here, and Jen. I love this place, always have, even when I had to get away from it. I think I started to remember when we delivered Gorgeous."

They were good reasons, but Lily's heart sank, knowing that she wasn't included in any of them. Emptiness opened up inside her. Never in her life had she felt so utterly left out.

"You're not going, then."

"No."

"You might have told me that the other day." She lifted her chin, torn between wanting to cry with relief that he wasn't going and fear that he would want more from her than she could give. She knew it was unreasonable and unfair. She knew it made no sense to want him to stay when her heart still quaked when she thought of marriage.

"And would it have made any difference?"

The quiet question struck her with the precision of an arrow. Would it? If he had come right out and said he was planning on staying in Larch Valley indefinitely, would her answer have been different? She would have her life, her job, her friends. No moving around, none of the weeks alone while he was away. And then she pictured herself standing at the front of the church, as Jen had with Andrew, and her chest contracted as panic threaded through her.

Noah boosted himself away from the sawhorse and came to stand in front of her. Her breaths shallowed at the mere nearness of him. Her fingers itched to reach out and touch him, to gather the light cotton of his T-shirt in her hands. "I tried to tell you what I'd decided, but you didn't want to listen. You were so afraid, so bent on pushing me away that I knew."

"Knew what?" She dared a glance upward, into his eyes. Saw his jaw tighten as he clenched his teeth. Her gaze dropped to his lips and for a moment he seemed to lean closer. Then his expression changed, just a hint of sympathy entering his eyes as he withdrew the slightest little bit.

"Knew that you were too afraid to say yes."

Her eyebrows shot toward her hairline as the spell surrounding them broke. "How could I know you were staying here? Yes, I was afraid! You were asking me to leave my home behind, my job! My life that I've built here!"

"I was asking you to share your life with me, Lily."

She turned away from the earnestness in his

eyes. Took several deep breaths, trying to calm the frantic beating of her heart. She had desperately wanted to share herself with a man before, and it had gone so very wrong. Love was one thing. And she did love him. How could she not? But marriage, that was quite another. The act of giving your life to one person for safekeeping forever. Or until they decided to hand it back to you.

"You're scared." Noah came forward and spun her around with his hand. "The idea of marriage scares you to death, I know that. I knew that when I asked you! Don't you think I'm scared? Do you know how hard it was to tell you I loved you?"

"I'm sorry it was such a burden!" Her eyes flashed up at him. Why did she continually feel as though she was an obligation? She needed him to share his life with her, as well. If only he could see that!

"Don't do that!" he yelled, exasperated. "That's not it at all, and you know it!"

"I can't let myself love you, don't you see that?"

He gave her arm a little shake. "Look at me, Lily. I've done nothing but think about how I would support you. Worry about how my physical challenges might affect a relationship." He let go of her arm and ran his fingers through his hair. "Dammit, woman," he muttered, quieter now. "I wasn't even sure how to hold you on the dance floor. How would I manage making love?"

The backs of her eyes stung at his honest admission. She'd known all along about his insecurities. "Do you really think I care about any of that?" Her voice was raspy, raw with all the emotions she was trying to hold back.

"I worried about it and I asked you anyway. Because I thought you trusted me. But I realized something even more important. I realized that this had nothing to do with me being in the forces or working Lazy L. This has to do with you and what you're really afraid of."

A knot tightened, grew in Lily's core. Afraid? Hell yes, she was afraid. She'd never wanted this. Never wanted to feel so strongly again. Never wanted to be tempted to throw it all away for the love of one person. She'd sworn she'd never do it again. She'd had to keep reminding herself that he was temporary. She'd felt safe in knowing it. But now he wasn't temporary, and somehow the fear remained.

"You want love with boundaries, Lil. It was

okay when you knew I'd be leaving again. I thought so, too. When I first got here, all I wanted was to get better and get back to the regiment."

"What changed?" Lily chanced a look up, feeling moisture on her cheeks but ignoring it.

"You changed me. You made me look at things differently. I told you things I hadn't talked about with anyone ever. You helped me when I needed it but let me stand on my own two feet, too, like the day we delivered the foal." He lifted his hand and grazed her cheek with a finger. "You made me feel like a man again."

"Noah, don't…" Her voice broke on the last word, but he persisted, his soft voice relentless. He cupped her cheek.

"I was safe when I was going away. It's not marriage that you doubt, Lily. Your problem is that you don't believe in love. Not the forever kind."

He leaned forward and kissed her forehead gently. "The kind I want to give to you."

Lily savored the touch of his lips on her forehead before forcing herself to back away. Was he right? Was that the nagging feeling that she couldn't escape?

"Maybe I don't," she confessed. She pressed her hands to her hot cheeks for a moment, trying to find the words to explain all that she needed, wanted. "Maybe I don't believe in it because I've never seen it."

And then it was like beams of light into her mind and heart. That was it, wasn't it. The reason why Jasmine had never settled on one man. The reason why she'd moved from relationship to relationship, taking Lily with her. She'd simply been searching and coming up empty. Looking for the mate to complete the other half of her soul and never finding him. The reason why she'd been so flippant about Lily's relationship with Curtis, insisting it wasn't real.

And she'd been right. She'd been right because the real thing was standing before her right now and she knew what he was offering wasn't enough. That was what she was afraid of. Not of loving him. She couldn't help but love him. But that one day he'd realize he'd made a mistake and it would be over. That *his* love wouldn't be forever.

She fled the tack room, needing to get out of the dark corners and into the sunshine where she could breathe. She had to find the words to tell him what she wanted. If she could even consider jumping into love—into marriage—it needed to be on her terms.

She just had to be strong enough to ask for it.

His boots sounded on the concrete and she wiped her eyes, trying desperately to ignore the uncertainty rolling around in her stomach. She could do this. She sniffled, straightening her shoulders. For the first time, something mattered more than protecting herself. She could say the words. She could ask for what she deserved. The way she'd never been able to face up to anyone she'd loved ever before.

He stopped at the edge of the barn, in the breach of the door just behind her.

And when she turned to face him, it was with eyes that saw the man she loved, the man she would always love.

"Noah, I love you."

In a split second he had her pulled tight against his chest. He kissed the top of her head, bathed in the warmth of the sun. She returned his embrace, knowing they needed this as a starting point. Needed to let their love be the foundation for everything else, if they had any hope of making it work.

"But you have to listen to me." She pushed back, putting her hands on his upper arms in a way she wouldn't have dared only a few short weeks ago. "Because we can't go on this way. You're right about one thing, I am scared. I'm terrified. I'm scared because I can't go through life being invisible."

"I see you," he replied, bending his knees slightly so that their eyes were level. "I see a woman who is caring, and compassionate, and funny, and selfless…."

"That is just the outside! That is what I want people to see. Noah, I'm a woman who spent her life trying to please other people. The one time I tried to do something for myself was when I ran away with Curtis. And it went spectacularly wrong. And so the time has come for me to be selfish."

She looked into his eyes, praying for courage to say what she had to say. "I know the reason my mother kept us moving from place to place. She was searching for, and never finding the person she wanted to spend her life with. Oh, Noah, I would share all my life with you. But you have not shared with me. There are times I have felt so left out, so in the dark and feeling like I didn't know you at all."

"You know me better than anyone," he protested, and she felt her pulse give a little kick. But she had to stay on course.

"I knew the Noah that came home, the Noah that was wounded and the Noah who was working his way through healing. I shared things with you about myself because I felt I could trust you…and that did not come easy to me. I fought my feelings for you so much. I didn't want to love you, but I always knew you would be going away and I thought my heart was safe."

How wrong she'd been. The night she'd seen his body laid bare to her, she'd felt a love so big, so pure, it had changed everything. And she'd started to realize how little she truly knew about him. About his hopes and dreams, because he had kept so much hidden from her.

She reached out and took his hand, needing the connection as she gathered the strength to continue.

"When you showed up in your uniform, I thought you had come to say goodbye. Instead you proposed, and all I could see was a question mark. When would you be going back to duty? Where would we live? What would you be doing? How could I find a life again? I realized I had not once seen your uniform, although you had claimed that the army was the most important thing to you. I didn't know you were going to the funeral even though it could have easily come up in conversation. The most important thing in your life was the one thing you didn't share. Even the details of your injury…those are sketchy at best. The bits you allowed me to see." Emotion tore at her throat. "I can't live that way, Noah. I can't. I'm not strong enough. Or confident enough. I would always be wondering, waiting for the dream of being with you to end."

Noah took a step back, staggered by what Lily had said. Had he done that? Had he really shut her out? He thought back to their conversations, their moments together. Had he truly discussed his plans with her? His doubts about going back into an army where he didn't fit anymore? His longing to be with family? How he'd felt contented back at Lazy L in a way he hadn't expected?

He hadn't. And as they stood there in the summer sunshine, he realized that when he'd proposed, he'd asked her to take a leap with him when he'd barely made a single step himself.

He met her gaze and saw her eyes, wide and sorrowful, shining back at him. "You're right. I asked you to share my life without sharing mine with you."

She nodded.

He swallowed, wanting to explain how he'd felt, not sure if he could. Never in his whole life had he discussed his feelings this deeply. But he loved her. And he would do anything to put the smile back on her face. To feel her hand in his. That was more important than being afraid.

"I didn't think you loved me, you see," he began. "I kept telling myself you couldn't, not in my condition. I didn't know what the future would bring. All I knew was that I felt better—happier—when I was with you. But when the time came to decide what I wanted to do, I was selfish, Lily, and I was wrong. I tested you, and that wasn't fair. I had to know you loved me for me, not because I was staying in Larch Valley or because I was moving away to be a part of the service again. I've been married to the army my whole adult life. And suddenly it wasn't enough. I wanted *you*. I needed you to want me that much, too. I didn't want the rest to matter, and because of that I didn't see I was shutting you out. I'm sorry, Lily, so sorry. I never meant to exclude you."

"You left the army because of me?" Her voice was a tiny whisper.

"You see?" He ran his hand through his hair,

leaving the dark spikes standing on end. "I didn't want you to bear the responsibility of my choices. I never wanted you to feel I expected something of you. I didn't leave *for* you—I left *because* of you. Because you showed me there was more in my life than I imagined. You showed me the possibility of a new start. And one I prayed to God you might someday want to share."

He reached out, running his thumb over her cheek, touching her lips before letting his hand fit the curve of her neck. "I have never been in love before. After my parents, I was sure that it wasn't something I wanted. Even now, I see how lonely my mom is. I watched Dad's pain after she'd gone. Oh, Lily, you never trusted in a forever kind of love before. I'm here to say you don't have to. Just trust in me. I won't betray your faith. I promise."

The sob came out before she could stop it, a small hiccup of emotion as she wound her arms around him, holding him close. "I knew the night that we danced and you said you wanted to be perfect that I'd fallen for you."

"Before the wedding?"

"Oh, yes." She smiled against the fabric of his shirt, absorbing the feel of his unique shape against hers, the scent of him that was just Noah. "Saying no to you was the most difficult thing I've ever done."

"Harder than being left at the altar?" There was a note of incredulity in his voice. She nodded and peered up into his face.

"Absolutely. I never loved him the way I love you, Noah. If I didn't love you so much, I wouldn't have had the courage to say what I did today."

She knew as a concept that didn't make much sense, but it was true. Her love for him made her stronger. Gave her the desire to fight for the life she wanted.

Her heart clubbed at her ribs. His deep eyes were questioning, with just a hint of challenge that she adored.

It wasn't what she'd planned, wasn't what she'd envisioned, but something greater than logic propelled her to kneel before him, holding his left hand in hers, pressing a kiss to the work-roughened skin. "Noah," she said clearly, her voice ringing out into the summer air. "Will you marry me, Noah? Will you take me, with all of my faults, all of my weaknesses, all of my scars? Because I love you, Noah. More than I ever thought possible. It doesn't matter where we live. As long as we're together."

He tugged on her hand, lifting her to her feet. "Lily," he said gently, "do you know how many times you have humbled me? With your caring and compassion and strength. It would have been impossible for me not to have fallen in love with you."

Lily's eyes misted with tears. "Is that a yes?"

He laughed, a sound filled with happiness and emotion. "Yes, of course it is. I'll marry you. The sooner the better. I'll be damned if I'm letting you get away again."

He pulled her into his embrace, sealing the engagement with a kiss. "Definitely not letting you get away," he murmured against her mouth.

The clatter of footsteps interrupted the moment before an exclamation cut through the air. Lily's and Noah's heads turned together to see Jen and Andrew coming through the barn. Jen stopped abruptly, put a hand to her mouth.

"Drew! They're not…are they?"

Lily felt a giggle, a warm, expansive bubble of happiness rise within her. Noah's arm held firm around her waist as they faced Andrew and Jen together.

Jen rushed forward, her jaw slack with surprise, but elation beaming from her eyes. "When did this happen?"

Lily laughed, enjoying her friend's surprise. "Pretty much the morning you asked me to deliver those groceries," she admitted with a laugh.

"Lily's in the market for a matron of honor," Noah added, the smile Lily adored curling its way up his cheek.

"You're getting married? Oh, my word. And to think we were inside being worried..." She hugged Noah for the second time that day, before standing back and shaking her head, as if she still didn't quite believe it. "I hate the word *matron*, but this is one time I'll wear it. Gladly."

Andrew caught up with Jen and placed his hands on her shoulders. Happiness glowed from his face. "It's true? The two of you?"

Lily nodded, while Noah answered, "It took some work."

Andrew barked out a laugh while Jen rushed forward, claiming Lily in a hug this time. "Oh, you guys!" she wailed, stepping back and dabbing at her eyes. "And oh, Lily, just think, this time you'll be making your own wedding dress! It's so perfect."

Lily looked up at Noah, knowing Jen knew nothing about the dress still hanging in her closet. It was time to let it go. It was time to put the past behind her and look forward to a kind of future she'd only dreamed of. Noah's eyes glowed at her, strong and true, and she smiled.

"I've made the last wedding dress I'm ever going to," she announced, squeezing Noah's hand. "I think a shopping trip for something shiny and new is in order."

The two couples chatted happily about future plans until Jen stopped up short. "Wait a minute," she said, turning to Lily, her expression flat with mock seriousness. "I seem to recall it wasn't that long ago that you said you didn't date cowboys."

Lily grabbed Noah's hand and stepped on tiptoe to kiss his cheek, but he turned at the last second and caught her lips in a sweet, brief kiss.

She turned to Jen, now understanding why it was her friend seemed to glow from within all the time. She smiled, and curled into Noah's side.

"You know how it is," she remarked to Jen, while her gaze remained locked with Noah's. "I guess I'd just never met the right one."

MILLS & BOON PUBLISH EIGHT LARGE PRINT TITLES A MONTH. THESE ARE THE EIGHT TITLES FOR AUGUST 2010.

THE ITALIAN DUKE'S VIRGIN MISTRESS
Penny Jordan

THE BILLIONAIRE'S HOUSEKEEPER MISTRESS
Emma Darcy

BROODING BILLIONAIRE, IMPOVERISHED PRINCESS
Robyn Donald

THE GREEK TYCOON'S ACHILLES HEEL
Lucy Gordon

ACCIDENTALLY THE SHEIKH'S WIFE
Barbara McMahon

MARRYING THE SCARRED SHEIKH
Barbara McMahon

MILLIONAIRE DAD'S SOS
Ally Blake

HER LONE COWBOY
Donna Alward

MILLS & BOON PUBLISH EIGHT LARGE PRINT TITLES A MONTH. THESE ARE THE EIGHT TITLES FOR SEPTEMBER 2010.

ભ

VIRGIN ON HER WEDDING NIGHT
Lynne Graham

BLACKWOLF'S REDEMPTION
Sandra Marton

THE SHY BRIDE
Lucy Monroe

PENNILESS AND PURCHASED
Julia James

BEAUTY AND THE RECLUSIVE PRINCE
Raye Morgan

EXECUTIVE: EXPECTING TINY TWINS
Barbara Hannay

A WEDDING AT LEOPARD TREE LODGE
Liz Fielding

THREE TIMES A BRIDESMAID...
Nicola Marsh